PIGFACE AND THE PERFECT DOG

An Oak Grove Mystery
featuring Susan Hogan

Judy Alter

ALTER EGO PUBLISHING

Alter Ego Publishing
Fort Worth, TX 76110

ISBN 978-0-9990371-3-3 (digital)
ISBN 978-0-9990371-4-0 (trade paperback)

Editor: Lourdes Venard, Comma Sense Editing
Cover Art Design: Sherry Wachter
Interior Book Design: Jennifer Zaczek, Cypress Editing
Release Date: August 2017

Disclaimer: Oak Grove University is purely a creation of the author's imagination. Although set within easy distance of the Dallas/Fort Worth Metroplex, it is not meant to be any specific school within the North or Central Texas regions. Naturally, my knowledge of various schools in the area went into the creation of Oak Grove, but to make specific connections between it and a real university would be a mistake. And to place the murder herein on a specific campus would be a total mistake. Similarly, the characters in this book bear no relation to any real people, on or off Texas campuses.

For Kathie, Carol, and Subie—ladies of my heart

And for

*The Two Jeans, Walbridge and Chaffee, with thanks for
listening, loving, and being you*

Chapter One

Susan Hogan thought she was going to meet her maker that March day. Her first thought was irreverent. "Really, God? In a grocery store in Oak Grove? Have you got this wrong somehow?" After all, she reasoned, she'd missed death at the hands of Eric Lindler months ago, so why should she die now in a grocery store?

She'd been standing on one foot and then the other, trying to decide if Jake wanted T-bones or a big sirloin. If he couldn't go to the store himself, at least he could give better directions.

The butcher eyed her suspiciously. But then she had the feeling he was looking beyond her. That's when she felt something hard hit her shoulder—not a grocery cart, too high for that. She whirled and found herself staring at a man with a rifle slung over his shoulder, two belts of ammunition wrapped around his ample middle. Apparently, the rifle struck her as he turned. Accidentally or on purpose? She wasn't sure.

Susan's reaction was neither gentle nor slow. "What the hell are you doing in this store with that gun?"

The man glared at her, beady eyes blazing out of a puffy, pale face beneath a balding head with the remaining hair pulled back into a sparse ponytail. "It's not a gun, lady. It's a rifle. And I got a right to carry it. Got to protect myself." He bristled with defensive arrogance.

Susan realized by now he was probably not going to shoot her right then . . . or at least that's what she told herself. "You can't bring that into a grocery store where there are defenseless women and children." She hoped he knew that included her.

The butcher tried to distract her. "Uh, Doctor Hogan, your steaks?"

The man with the rifle snarled. "Doctor, huh? Someone from that college I bet, not a real doctor. Bet you're full of crazy ideas. But I'll tell you what, lady. The law says I can carry this in here."

As her adrenaline rush subsided, Susan found her hands shaking. She gave silent thanks and apologized to the Lord for her anger. Then she turned away from the man abruptly and ordered two T-bones, one small, one larger. Behind her she heard the man mutter.

"Don't mess with me, lady."

She wished with every bone in her body that Jake was with her. He wouldn't tolerate threats, and she was still convinced the man shouldn't have that weapon in the store. She didn't care if it was a rifle or a gun.

The butcher eyed her but remained noncommittal behind the safety of his chest-high counter. Susan was quite sure he didn't want to be shot either. Without ever looking again at the man with the rifle, she marched angrily toward the checkout counter, but with every step down the aisle of canned goods, she felt there was a bull's-eye on her back.

Susan managed to exchange polite talk with the cashier, but her inward thoughts were already railing at Jake, rehearsing all the things she would tell him. Having paid, she rushed out the door and jumped into her Toyota. It was battered and old, but it got her where she needed to go. Even after a bad experience, she still longed for the open freedom of Jake's motorcycle. After one wreck, he had forbidden her to ride it, even though the wreck wasn't her fault.

Pulling her cell phone out of the side pocket in her bag, she punched the number one on speed dial for Jake.

He answered with a gruff, "Phillips."

"Jake? I've got to tell you what I saw in the grocery store." She strained to make her voice sound normal, hiding her anger, and must have succeeded, because Jake was not impressed. "Susan, I don't give a damn what you saw in the grocery, not even if it was a vampire from outer space. Some rancher out west of town found a body in his pasture, and I suspect it's a student who's been reported missing. I've got to go out there, call the county sheriff, and hang around until he and his people get there." Jake was chief of campus police at Oak Grove University.

Susan Hogan put her head down on the steering wheel in frustration. Finally, she choked out a strident, "We've lost another one? No! It can't be."

The fall before a coed named Missy Jackson had been murdered, and Detective Dirk Jordan had been determined that Susan Hogan, professor of English, had done it because the girl's body was found in the trunk of her car. Susan lived several lifetimes and nearly did die before that was straightened out. Jake's words brought the whole incident flooding back into her mind.

"Will you have to deal with Dirk the Jerk Jordan again?" She remembered her anger at Lieutenant. Jordan.

"Probably not, though he may be called in. It's a county case, since it was outside town. But the missing boy is a town student, so an investigation may lead to some people who fall within Jordan's jurisdiction."

"Who's the boy?" Susan didn't know why but she dreaded the answer. She couldn't see Jake run his hand across his burr haircut and shrug his shoulders. But she knew the gesture well enough.

"Not saying until I get out there and confirm the identity. Maybe I won't know. I can't keep up with 10,000 students on this campus. I'll recognize him if he's someone who's been in trouble before. If it's the boy who's missing, I'll recognize him. Makes me sick to my stomach."

Not a cheerful thought, but Susan's mind was working again. "Who's the sheriff?"

"Walter Wainwright. Nice guy, usually."

"You'll be late, won't you? I'll save the steaks."

"Thanks. And, Susan, what happened in the grocery store?"

She took a deep breath. "Nothing. I'll tell you about it later."

"I love you," he said and was gone.

Susan sat in the car, processing what Jake had told her, wondering about a young boy who'd ended up dead in a West Texas pasture. When she looked up and prepared to pull out of the grocery store parking lot, she saw the man with the rifle walking away from the store, that belligerent scowl still on his face. Next to him was a slight man, with unkempt hair almost to his shoulders and a rifle flung over one shoulder. Susan gave them a look of distaste and wheeled away. Well, as fast as the aging car would wheel.

At home, Susan put the steaks in the fridge, along with the artichoke she almost forgot she'd bought, and then considered her dinner options. Dry cereal didn't much appeal, especially since there was no milk. She hadn't expected to go to the grocery until Jake texted asking her to get steaks. And she wasn't organized enough to have a grocery list.

I'll go to Aunt Jenny's. She'll always welcome me.

Aunt Jenny had raised Susan with love and kindness and strict rules after her mother died and her father threw up his hands at the thought of raising a daughter alone. He visited occasionally, bringing inappropriate gifts, and died when she was eight or nine. Aunt Jenny never said it, but Susan suspected he wore himself out drinking and chasing women. She adored Aunt Jenny almost as much as she loved Jake. When things were tough with Missy Jackson's murder, neither Jake nor Susan could dissuade Jenny Hogan from coming to Oak Grove to "take care of my Susan." That she might be a complication never occurred to Aunt Jenny, and Susan didn't have the heart to tell her. Aunt Jenny went to church, found a beau, retired Judge John Jackson, and decided she liked Oak Grove so well, she'd just stay.

* * * *

Now, Jenny Hogan sat in the living room of her small house near the center of Oak Grove, with the judge. As a matter of fact, she sat on his lap and leaned against him.

"I'm surely glad you decided to move down here," he said, bending his head just enough to plant a kiss on her forehead.

"You didn't mind going all the way to Wichita Falls to pack up my things and my cat?" she asked coyly. She knew the answer. This conversation was like a litany they repeated to each other.

"The cat may be a little bit much," he said, "but you're worth it. Always been a dog person, but I guess I can learn to live with a cat named Sybil."

Jenny Hogan sat up indignantly, hands on her hips as though outraged. "John Jackson, you're not living here. Sybil is."

"That may change some day," he said lightly and kissed her again, this time more soundly.

Jenny Hogan was a maiden lady, seventy-some years old, who'd never had time to marry because she had Susan to care for, and after that, well, it just seemed too late.

They were both startled when the front door opened and Susan burst in. She stopped mid-stride and asked, "Am I interrupting?"

Jenny was by then off the judge's lap, smoothing the apron she wore, and looking guilty as sin.

"Susan!" Jenny said. "We were just deciding whether to have broccoli or salad with our spaghetti." A blush brought roses to her cheeks that matched the roses blooming in the small but well-tended garden she'd inherited with the house.

She reached for a hug from Susan. They were a contrast, Jenny as short and round as Susan was tall and lanky. Jenny's gray hair was pulled back in a bun but now by the end of the day much of it had escaped confinement and cascaded down the back of her neck, with some wisps framing her face and giving her a winsome look. She wore a cotton dress under her clean and starched apron.

Susan's hair, kept blonde by deliberate effort, was cut short and spiky, and she wore jeans fashionably torn at the knee and a man's shirt she'd stolen from Jake, its tail hanging loosely. She bent to give Jenny a hug and an affectionate kiss on the cheek.

"I vote for salad, and I'll make it, after I get myself a glass of wine. That is if I may stay for supper." Susan turned to the judge and gave him a hug that was only slightly less effusive than what she'd bestowed on her aunt.

Aunt Jenny didn't drink—Jake's one attempt to give her medicinal bourbon had been disastrous—but she kept Scotch for the judge, beer for Jake, and wine for Susan. "Of course, Susan. We're delighted that you're here. Where's Jake?"

Susan tried to be offhand and lighthearted about it, but she apparently didn't pull it off well. "He got called out west of town."

"Boy found in a pasture?" the judge asked. He had risen from the couch to greet Susan and now followed the two women to the kitchen.

"How did you know?"

"I still have sources, Susan." His tone was benevolent, but he didn't really answer her question.

The doorbell rang, and the judge headed for the door. "You expecting more company, Jenny?" He might have been in his early eighties, but he still walked erectly, his head held high as his long steps swallowed the distance to the front door.

"Oh," Aunt Jenny said, trying to tie her apron with one hand and soothe her flyaway hair with the other, "that's Gus. He's bringing my surprise."

A young man stood at the door, early twenties at most, in jeans and a polyester shirt with the insignia of a grocery store on its pocket. With one arm that sported a dragon tattoo, he clutched a gangly puppy, one of those adorable babies that would grow into a huge dog. Its feet were already big. "It's Miss Hogan's dog, sir. Her name is Lucy."

"Fiddlesticks! Who ever heard of a dog named Lucy?" the judge said. But he reached out a practiced hand for the pup to sniff and then expertly took the dog, examining its feet, tossing its ears.

"I named her," Aunt Jenny said quietly. "She looks like a Lucy. See how she cocks her head at me when I call her name?" Then she explained that Gus had carried her groceries to the car and, as he loaded them into the passenger seat, told her about the dog he was hiding in a neighbor's garage. The puppy needed a real home, and Gus was concerned.

The judge groaned, and Susan held her breath. Aunt Jenny surely wouldn't approve of that tattoo. Susan was sure she'd thank the young man and dismiss him, but instead she invited him in. Reaching out to take the puppy from the judge, Jenny said, "Gus, you come right in and get comfortable. Susan will get you a cold drink, won't you, dear?" And with that she began to babble to the dog, talking baby talk, calling her "My baby" and referring to herself in the third person as "Mama."

The judge followed Susan to the kitchen to strengthen his drink and roll his eyes at her. Gus followed to ask, "Could I have a beer?"

Susan almost dropped her wine glass. "A beer? I'm sorry, but you aren't old enough, are you?" Any kid who sacked groceries was not twenty-one. She was sure of it.

Gus looked at the floor, shy and embarrassed, and said, "I'm twenty-two." To back up his assertion, he added, "I'm an assistant manager at the store." He looked down at the badge he wore on his shirt.

Susan wasn't about to ask for his driver's license. She gave him one of Jake's Samuel Adams beers and poured herself a glass of chardonnay, noticing that the judge had put a really healthy slug of Scotch in his glass.

"Jenny, that is a dog, not a baby," the judge said in a strict tone. "You'll have to treat her as a dog, or she'll be unbearable."

"She's just a baby," Jenny protested, clutching the dog even closer.

The judge took a deep breath. "I'm too old to train a puppy," he said to no one.

"Oh, I'll train her." Aunt Jenny held the now-wriggling puppy as though she would allow no one to snatch her away, not even Judge John Jackson.

"How many puppies have you trained?" he asked, knowing the answer full well.

She ignored him and turned to Gus. "Why does she have this thick, ugly collar? It's way too heavy for a little girl like this. I'm going to throw it away."

Judge Jackson raised his hand. "Wait, Jenny, until we get her a suitable collar." Turning to Gus, he asked, "Do you have a leash?"

"In the truck," the boy said. "I'll go get it."

He returned with a thick rope with a heavily padded leather loop for a handle.

"That's too heavy for her too!" Aunt Jenny exclaimed.

Judge Jackson agreed but said, "Give it to me just in case. Jenny, we'll go shopping for . . . ah, Lucy . . . tomorrow in Fort Worth."

Mollified, Aunt Jenny went back to crooning to the puppy, who reached up to lick her face. The other three stared at the sight with varying kinds of astonishment.

Jenny Hogan had never had a dog. When Susan was a child, Aunt Jenny said they didn't belong in apartments, and she didn't have time to care for one. They'd had cats. Jenny still did. Sybil lurked somewhere, avoiding the inevitable meeting with a dog.

Asked why he was giving the dog to Aunt Jenny, Gus delivered a rather vague story about finding it abandoned in the country and knowing his father wouldn't let him keep it. His dad didn't like dogs, said they brought nothing but trouble, and threatened to run off any Gus brought home by using pepper spray on them. Gus, on the other hand, loved dogs and hid the puppy in the neighbor's garage until he could find a home for her.

"And Aunt Jenny?" Susan asked, thinking her aunt was the most unlikely candidate ever.

"I happened to carry her groceries out for her today—sack boys were all busy—and she seemed like such a nice lady, I told her about the puppy while I loaded the groceries into her car. I guess I got carried away, but the more I talked, the more interested she became. Finally, she told me the puppy's name was Lucy, which startled me because I hadn't named her yet. Then she said I should bring it to her tonight, so here I am."

Jenny cradled the puppy with satisfaction, cooing to her.

Susan's first thought was, *Wait till Jake hears this story*. Then, of course, she thought of Jake out in that pasture, keeping a dead boy company. And the grocery store. Had Aunt Jenny encountered any men with rifles? This wasn't the time to ask.

Gus joined them for spaghetti. Jenny would listen to no protests, though she was so preoccupied with Lucy that Susan dished up the dinner.

Gus lost a little of his shyness as they talked. Lucy wanted to join them too, but the judge was firm that if she was fed from the table once, she'd be a beggar forever. When she piddled on the floor, Aunt Jenny jumped up and said, "No, oh, no."

The judge simply scooped up the dog and took her outside. "She'll get the idea pretty soon," he said when they came back. Later, he went home to retrieve a crate he'd used with one of his dogs. Aunt Jenny protested that it was cruel to put a dog in a crate, but he said, "She'll feel safer in her own space and you'll sleep better not worrying about what she's chewing on. We'll get her some toys tomorrow."

Susan addressed the older man. "Judge, I didn't know you knew so much about dogs." He didn't have a dog, and the idea hadn't occurred to Susan.

"Used to raise hunting dogs. Like them a lot. I been thinking about getting another dog, but now I guess I won't have to. I have one. I think she's maybe four months old." He rumpled Lucy's ears affectionately.

Gus thanked Jenny profusely for the delicious spaghetti and for taking the dog. As he left, the judge said, "Give your folks my best. You don't have to tell that father of yours we met over a dog."

After Gus left, Jenny demanded to know who his father was and how the judge knew him.

"Buster Conroy. Owns the best mechanic shop in town. Known him forever. He used to raise and train hunting dogs. Good at it too. Had some wonderful dogs. I bought at least two from him. But one night years ago someone with a mighty grudge against Buster went to his kennel and shot every one of those dogs. Never did find out who did it or why. Might have been a difference over a car repair. But since that night, Buster's been death on dogs and guns. Don't ever mention either one to him."

* * * *

Susan left shortly after Gus. On the way home her thoughts were jumbled, and she feared sleep would bring pictures of men with rifles and dead dogs, a body in a pasture, and Aunt Jenny cradling a pup. *Who was the boy and why was he in the pasture? Oak Grove University treasured its reputation as a safe, small school. Only now there had been two murders in one academic year. What was happening in her safe little world?*

11

Chapter Two

Tom Donley was waiting for Jake when he pulled up to the Donley ranch house. "Hate to bring you out on a call like his," he said apologetically, coming forward with his hand extended for a shake.

Jake took the hand and said, "Not as bad as I hate to come. You call the sheriff?"

"Yeah, he's on his way. Don't like attracting all this attention to my place. And Lord knows his crew will tear up my pasture looking for clues. Damn shame about that boy."

Jake nodded. "You recognize him?"

"Nope. All those college kids look alike to me. Cows aren't in that pasture, and I'd never of found that boy if Scooby hadn't raised a terrible fuss." Scooby, a farm collie of uncertain heritage but determined spirit, circled Tom's legs, giving off an occasional yip as his master talked. "Dog would run out there and then come back barkin' his fool head off to get me to go with him. Finally, I did. But I couldn't tell nothin' except that it was a body, looked to be a young boy. Face down, and I didn't want to touch it. Knew anyway I shouldn't."

"Take me out there." Jake couldn't have put his dread into words.

The two men walked in silence, apparently having exhausted all conversation that they needed. Donley was not a man given to small talk, and Jake was lost in his own thoughts, wondering what kind of hell was going to explode on the campus after this latest death.

The ground was still bare and brown from winter as they scuffed through dry weeds and grass. No bluestem yet, none of the wild prairie grasses that Donley so carefully nurtured on his land, but prickly pear was plentiful, along with clumps of old mesquite and mongrel bushes and dried cow patties. Their feet stirred up small clouds of dust—as always, West Texas was in a drought. Overhead, the sky was blue and cloudless, but Jake spotted a hawk circling around a spot farther on and thought they best get to the body before the birds and critters did.

The boy's body lay in a shallow spot, as though the earth had carved out a small place for it. A bullet hole was evident between the shoulder blades, and the boy lay in a puddle of dried and drying blood. As he stood and stared, Jake knew it was who he had suspected and feared: Jesse Conroy, Buster Conroy's youngest son, a town student at the college. Jake shook his head; he knew this boy only too well. Beside him lay a rifle.

Jesse Conroy went to school on a scholarship and could have been student body president, outstanding scholar, anything he wanted. But he chose hijinks and chasing girls . . . and causing more than a bit of trouble. Jake remembered thinking that he'd have had a lot more trouble with Jesse if the boy lived on campus, but he lived at home with his parents—though he often bunked with this or that friend in the dorms. Far as Jake knew, he'd never been caught staying overnight in a girl's room but he bet Jesse tried. Mostly, he'd clashed with Jake over parking tickets, which Jesse ignored, and public drinking in campus parking lots. But there was that one time, when a fight broke out, that he'd found Jesse carrying a concealed handgun, strictly forbidden on campus. Jake saw to it that the boy was suspended and earned Jesse's undying hatred. Not that hatred mattered now.

The two men stood, shuffling their feet, staring wordlessly at the body, and then looking away uncomfortably. Jake was relieved when the sheriff came . . . and doubly relieved that it would be the sheriff's duty to tell Buster Conroy his youngest son was dead.

Sheriff Wainwright walked up with a brisk stride, more used to dead bodies than either Jake or Donley. "What are you doing here, Jake? You usually don't horn in on my murders."

Jake shifted uncomfortably. "Got an anonymous call. Said one of our students had been shot, gave me pretty good directions to the spot."

"You didn't trace the call? What kind of voice?"

Jake felt he was being interrogated. "Phone company confirmed what I suspected. Throwaway cell phone but the call was placed on campus. Here's the odd thing: it was a girl on the phone."

The sheriff studied the body. "Buster Conroy's youngest boy, isn't it? You know him?"

Jake nodded. "'Fraid I do. He's had a few scrapes with my guys. I had to call him in once or twice. Got him suspended once for concealed carry on campus."

"Wonder if he had a girlfriend," the sheriff mused aloud.

"Last I knew he was after all the girls," Jake said, "but I'd have to ask around."

"You do that. Conroy's not gonna be easy to deal with."

Wainwright would have to wait for the coroner and his crew, but Jake figured maybe he could sneak away. "Can I turn this over to you now? I'll have to report to the provost and write up a report."

"Do all that tomorrow," Wainwright said. "You stay here as my backup. Any questions come up, you can swear I did everything by the book."

Jake was hungry, and he wanted some Scotch. He thought about Susan and the steaks, and wondered what she was doing. It would be a long night for him. He noticed Donley had quietly taken his dog and slipped away.

The coroner arrived. Doctor Leticia Hornsby. Jake had never met her, but he'd heard good things about her—efficient, easy to work with, pleasant. *Why,* he thought, *would a woman like that want to examine and cut up dead bodies?* It was beyond him. Tish, as those who knew her called her, got right to work, merely nodding at the men. By then, dark was coming on, and Hornsby's assistants set up huge floodlights that created an eerie scene in the dark pasture.

Jake felt himself shivering. It was late March, and a chill crept in with the darkness. He wished he'd worn a heavier jacket, but it had been almost warm this afternoon when he left the office.

Doctor Hornsby worked fast, calling soft requests to co-workers, handling the body gently and with respect but inspecting carefully.

There wasn't much for Jake and Walter Wainwright to talk about, but Jake didn't really want to watch the coroner at work.

When she finished and walked away from the body, Hornsby's conclusion was as expected. Jesse Conroy had been shot in the back. "Cowardly," Doctor Leticia Hornsby said. "Probably the rifle next to the body. We'll have to match bullets."

As she stripped off her gloves, she shook Jake's hand with the strength of a man and said, "Guess we haven't run into each other. Pleasure to meet you, but I wish it hadn't been over the body of a young boy in a field."

Jake hadn't realized she was black and wondered even more how she ended up in this part of Texas doing what she did. Some instinct told him she and Susan would get along great.

The coroner's crew put the body on a gurney, packed up their lights, and loaded everything into the van they'd driven up close. They offered Jake and Wainwright a ride back to their cars, but Jake preferred to walk. At least he'd thought to bring a flashlight. Walking even the half-mile back to his car might work some of the kinks out of his body—and his brain. Why was the boy shot and the rifle left beside him?

On the drive back to Oak Grove, he debated where to go for the night. Usually when he was upset about something— and he was upset about this murder—he went to his house out in the country, his refuge that he'd fitted just for him. But tonight, he craved the comfort of Susan—she could be both comforting and wise, when she wasn't being prickly, and he needed that tonight. He turned his Jeep toward her house.

Jake let himself in the sliding doors quietly and switched on the light over the stove so the overhead light wouldn't wake Susan—she was a light sleeper and some-times cranky when something woke her up. An empty wine glass in the sink told him she might be sleeping more soundly than usual. The clock said just after midnight.

He was fixing himself a nightcap—that good Scotch he saved for special occasions and, by God, this was one—

when Susan wandered in wearing a T-shirt and underpants. "Nice outfit," he said. His eyes crinkled. "That my T-shirt?"

"Uh-huh. Want it back right now?"

He shook his head and sat down heavily on a stool by the counter. "Nope, I'm not in the mood."

She got a glass of ice water and came to sit by him, careful not to reach out and touch him. "Tell me about it. Did you know the student?"

"Yeah. Unfortunately, I did. Town kid, always in trouble. Likeable enough, even sort of charming, at least with the girls, but just couldn't stay out of mischief and a few things worse. Name's Jesse Conroy. His dad runs the best mechanic shop in town. I've taken my Jeep there."

"Conroy!" Susan almost shouted the name. "I met his brother tonight. Kid named Gus, works as an assistant manager at Market Central, where Aunt Jenny shops."

He was mildly interested, enough to ask, "How'd you meet him?"

When Susan told him about Gus and Lucy and Aunt Jenny, Jake smiled for the first time since morning. "Aunt Jenny with a dog? A big dog at that? You're kidding, Susan. We can't let her do that. She's got no clue about training a dog, and if it's going to be as big as you say, it'll pull her down. We don't need a broken hip."

"I think it's going to be at least half the judge's next dog. He's apparently always had dogs until recent years, knows how to train them, and loves them. He wants Aunt Jenny to stop calling Lucy her baby and referring to herself as her mama."

"Thwarted maternal instincts?" he asked and almost laughed. "Wish I'd been there." There was a pause and then, more solemnly, "Yeah. I wish I'd been there instead of where I was." He downed the last of his Scotch and held out a hand. "Let's go to bed. I don't want to talk about it."

Later, as they lay in bed, close but not touching, he said wistfully, "I've been thinking how much I want a dog."

"You're not home enough."

"It could live here with you, and I'd train it and take care of it."

It was a long controversy between them. Neither would give up their home to move in with the other. Susan loved her ranch-style house, just big enough for her . . . and probably one other person if Jake wanted to move in. Jake, though, was attached to his home out in the country, the refuge he'd carefully remodeled to his exact taste and needs before he met Susan.

As she fell asleep, Susan thought, *Two dogs in my life? Please, Lord, no.*

* * * *

When Susan woke up Saturday morning, about eight, Jake was gone, and his side of the bed cool. When she wandered into the kitchen, she saw the note he'd left. "Call you later. Lunch?"

After coffee and toast, she gathered her determination and sat at her desk, her laptop in front of her and her research notes spread all over the desk. She was in the soggy middle of her manuscript on Zane Gray, knew where it was going but wasn't sure how to get it there. And this morning her thoughts wandered to the dead boy in the pasture and then to the grocery store gun guys.

Where's Jake and what's he doing? Why doesn't he call?

She squirmed in her seat, got another cup of coffee, and wrote three sentences. *At this rate, I might finish this before I retire but not in time for tenure next year.* Her thoughts clearly were not on Zane Grey. *Who were the men with rifles?*

Aunt Jenny rescued her, though it was a questionable rescue at best. She called about ten. "Oh, my, Susan, I suppose you've heard. John told me that young boy killed yesterday was Gus' brother. I don't know how John always knows what's going on, but he does. What should I do—a sympathy call doesn't seem right since I don't know the family. It would be intruding. And I don't know Gus that well at all, but I want him to know I'm grieving with him."

When Aunt Jenny paused for breath, Susan jumped into the conversation. "I think Jake would tell you not to do anything. If there's a memorial indicated in the obituary, you can send a small gift. And next time you see Gus, go out of your way to give him a hug."

"Oh, what a sensible girl you are, Susan. That's just what I'll do. I . . . wait, Lucy, don't chew on that. Bad girl!" She disappeared for a moment but came back to report that Lucy was chewing on an electrical cord.

"Aunt Jenny, you've got to get her chew toys. She could be electrocuted or choke on something she swallowed. Dog ownership is a big responsibility." She sounded preachy and knew it.

"The judge is taking us—that is Lucy and me—to Fort Worth this afternoon. We're going to buy some toys at the pet store and go to a training class. And Lucy needs dishes and a good leash and a proper collar—she has that big old leather thing that's far too thick for a young dog. I'm going to throw it away."

"How did you sleep last night?"

"Oh, Susan, I swear I didn't sleep a wink. I listened for her all night. And I had to let her out three times. I always told you when you were a child that owning a dog is a lot of trouble. But she's so sweet. She gives me kisses, and I just love her to death."

Susan hung up thinking it was a good thing her aunt had Lucy to take her mind off the death of Gus' brother.

Jake finally called after she'd written three paragraphs and thumbed through her notes so many times she'd see them in her sleep. "Pick you up in about thirty minutes. I got some hamburger, and I'll grill for us at my house. Okay?"

Of course, she said yes and then went to change into an oversized shirt meant for women and not Jake's hand-me-down she'd slept it. Not an advocate of makeup, she dusted a bit of powder and blush on and let it go at that. Then she ran her hands through her spiky short hair.

Jake was silent on the five-mile drive to his house, and Susan watched him covertly out of the corner of her eye. He kept his eyes on the road without even glancing at her, and she sensed he didn't want to talk. Once at the house he busied himself slicing tomatoes and onions, shaping hamburgers, pouring her a glass of wine and opening a beer for himself. As he worked, he finally talked.

"Spent most of the morning trying to find out if Jesse Conroy had a girlfriend. No leads so far. Nobody in the girls' dorms would talk to me, and I don't care to go near the family."

"Why not?"

"Buster Conroy's difficult. No telling how he'll take the news, and it's not my job to investigate. I'm stretching my involvement by investigating on campus, though Wainwright talked about deputizing me. I suppose he could do that—not sure if the university would like it."

"Why do you think there's a girlfriend?"

"I don't really. He was known on campus as a skirt chaser, but it was a girl who called and told me where to find Jesse's body. Hung up before I could ask any more.

Called from a throwaway cell phone but a trace placed it on campus, so that makes it legitimately my business—sort of."

"You're really upset about this, aren't you?"

He stopped slicing and chopping and leaned on the large part of the kitchen island, spreading his hands out and looking down. "Yeah, I'm upset. I was upset about Missy Jackson, but this is different. I didn't know her, and you were involved. As for Jesse, I knew him, and I probably could have saved him. I knew he was trouble, and all I did was discipline. I didn't help. I don't think I'll ever forget." He hung his head and wouldn't look at her.

She had no words of consolation. Guilt is an awful burden.

Suddenly, he looked straight at her and said, "Tell me everything about the men with the rifles in the grocery store."

"Why is that suddenly important?"

"Because a rifle, probably the one that shot him, was left next to his body. That's odd, to say the least. Doctor Hornsby, Tish, dusted it, of course, and found only Jesse's fingerprints. But he was shot in the back. I talked to Tish this morning. And by the by, I think you two should meet. You'd really mesh. Now tell me about the men."

While Susan talked about the men in the grocery store, recalling the one who looked like a porcine character, she named him Pigface. Jake grilled on his indoor Jenn-Air grill, but he was listening intently. Her description dwelt on the physical appearance of the two men, their attitude, everything she could scrounge out of memory about them. It wasn't what Jake wanted.

"Tell me about their guns."

She threw her hands up in the air and then began pacing. "I'm no gun expert, as you well know. All I can tell you is they were black and scary, slung around their shoulders with leather straps."

"Strings of ammo around the waist?"

"Yeah, definitely. How can you tell one black rifle from another?"

He almost laughed. "These guys, and some of their women, carry what are called black rifles—civilian versions of military weapons. They have black fiberglass stocks and blackened barrels. That's the kind of gun found next to Jesse, and judging from fingerprints, it was his gun. Don't know if that means he was involved with these wing nuts in town or just happened to have it."

Susan shook head. "You lost me, but I guess that's what guns they had. Looked like something a military man might have."

"Exactly," he crowed. And then he sobered. "Those two guys you saw aren't the only ones in town. I've heard reports of up to ten sightings. Thing is, far as I can figure, none of the people involved are from Oak Grove. And that includes the two women who seem sort of like camp followers. They sure have nothing to do with the university. So, what are they doing here?"

Susan told him how the one rifleman had sneered at her for being from the university. "He heard the butcher call me doctor," she explained. "Why do they think it's okay to go into stores and walk around with assault weapons?"

Jake told her about the open-carry demonstrations in bigger cities, with people flaunting their weapons and claiming they were only doing it to make people comfortable with guns and let them know how safe they are. "Safe!" he said sarcastically. "Did you read about the schools that arm teachers—one shot himself in the foot and another shot herself in the fanny. This whole idea of guns everywhere is unbelievable. If well-trained citizens—which those teachers obviously weren't—want guns to protect themselves, they should have them. But open carry of assault rifles?" He collapsed back into his seat. "It's legal, because hunters have to be allowed to carry their rifles. Should be a distinction between hunters and wing nuts, but I guess some people fit into both categories. The ones who scare me are the ones who say they have to carry for their own protection. In a grocery store? Give me a break!"

Susan thought she'd contribute. "I saw a picture on Facebook of a little girl holding one of those rifles, only it was pink, like it had been made for a girl. She was holding a dead rabbit. She was maybe seven at the most and had the saddest look on her face."

"Don't get me started on children and guns! That they even make pink rifles for little girls is a horrifying symbol of the gun culture. I tell you, this country has lost its mind."

"Do they really want to show how safe guns are?"

"No!" He almost shouted. "They want to show their contempt for rules; they want to flaunt their freedom to carry guns—and their contempt for the government. And they like the sense of power it gives them. A lot of it has to do with hate. Protestors are too often white supremacists. Some people, especially those who hate and need to feel superior, get swept up in it, but I'm afraid there's a small but hard core that's manipulating the whole thing. Question is, what are they doing in Oak Grove? I'd like to know where they're staying, where they're working, if they are. I want to know what they do every day."

"And you think the Conroy boy was mixed up in it?"

Jake shook his head slowly. "He was always ready for a new adventure, and I think he got in over his head."

"The judge said his father wouldn't allow guns in their house."

"So maybe there you have it. He was flaunting his freedom from his father. I can't help but suspect that some hotheaded open-carry guy shot him. But why leave the rifle next to his body?" He threw his hands up in the air and exclaimed, "I'm tired of talking about it." They ate their burgers in silence, and then he held a hand out to Susan and led her to the bedroom.

They spent the afternoon in bed. Later Susan reflected that for all the anger pent up inside him, he was amazingly gentle. After they slept for a while, she roused him to remind him about the steaks in her refrigerator.

* * * *

In a girls' dormitory on the Oak Grove campus, a young girl stood naked before a full-length mirror. Turning sideways, she studied her profile carefully. Then she sighed and pulled on a robe. Amanda Meyer was grateful that her roommate, Jill Ryan, had gone home for the weekend. Jill lived two hours away. Amanda could much more easily have gone home—it was only about eight blocks away. But she relished the solitude. She had a lot to think about.

Amanda pulled her too-curly hair back into a ponytail and secured it with a scrunchy, wishing she had glossy, straight blonde hair like some of the most popular girls on campus. As it was, her hair was black, and she always felt she was too chubby. The terry robe she had pulled around her did nothing to dispel that image. Even when she'd studied herself in the mirror, she'd seen short and chubby, not long, lean, and lithe.

She stared at the phone as though willing it to ring. *Where is Jesse? He promised to call ... yesterday. Said he had some business to take care of but he'd call by dinnertime.*

Dinnertime had come and gone, and Amanda had spent a long sleepless night, trying hard not to disturb Jill, not to let her know how troubled she was. Occasionally, a sigh or a sob would escape, but Jill slept on.

Friday morning Amanda made the effort, dressed for class in a pair of shorts and a T-shirt, grabbed her binder, and headed off to a morning-long biology lab. If they had to dissect a fetal pig today, she didn't think she was up to it. Just before she left, Jill said she was going home, and Amanda hoped her sigh of relief didn't show.

As soon as lab was over, Amanda hurried back to her room. She'd really thought she'd throw up, not once but three times, as they began work on their fetal pigs. That "project," if that's what you could call it, would last the rest of the semester, and she dreaded it, knew it would get worse with every swipe of her scalpel. In her room, she drank 7-Up, too tired, distraught, and nauseated to think about lunch.

Now, in the evening, she sat staring at her cell phone, as though she could will Jesse to call. It didn't work, and finally she lay down, drifting off into a light doze. When her cell phone did ring, she scrambled to find it in the bed. "Hello?"

"Amanda, it's Gus. Have you heard from Jesse in the last twenty-four hours?"

Her hand gripped the phone so tightly it hurt, but she tried to sound casual. "No, why?"

"I haven't been able to find him since yesterday morning. We usually talk once a day and, well, I'm worried. I thought maybe you'd talked to him."

"Jesse says he's through with me," she said, her voice dull. She'd known Jesse and Gus all her life, or so it seemed, and she didn't mind spilling that much truth to Gus. There were other things she wouldn't tell him.

Gus' voice wavered. "Amanda, you know he doesn't mean that. You two . . . well, you've been sweethearts since you were six."

"Yeah," she said, and bitterness crept into her voice, "but there weren't a lot of skinny blondes with shimmery straight hair around until this year."

Silence while Gus thought about what to say. Finally, "Can I do anything for you? Come get you for a beer? Maybe a late-night snack?"

Good old Gus. Worried about his brother, but he has time to worry about me. Jesse would never do that. All Jesse thinks about is Jesse. "Thanks, Gus. I really appreciate it, but I'm just going to go to sleep. Call me if you hear from Jesse."

"You got it," he said and punched the button to end the conversation.

Amanda Meyer cried herself to sleep. In the morning, her face was red and swollen, her eyes puffy, and she threw up twice. She needed to make herself presentable enough to go get something to eat.

Chapter Three

Jake and Susan had barely gotten to her house when the judge's Cadillac, old but shining with fresh polish, pulled into the driveway. He, Aunt Jenny, and Lucy—on a new, lightweight fabric leash—came in the sliding glass door from the deck, Lucy doing pretty well on the leash for a pup, though she occasionally turned to take it in her mouth. The pink collar around her neck sported rhinestones.

Aunt Jenny wore a go-to-church outfit and carried a matching purse. The judge was complete with coat and tie, and it struck Susan as funny that they'd dressed for a trip to the Fort Worth pet store as though it were a major occasion. She knew women her aunt's age who wore jeans and T-shirts, but not Aunt Jenny. Susan suppressed her smile.

"I thought she needed some bling," Aunt Jenny explained. "And pink is for girls, isn't it, my baby girl?" The last was, of course, directed to Lucy, who fixed Aunt Jenny with an adoring gaze. "Yes, baby, I'm going to throw away that nasty old collar you had."

"And I'll pull it out of the trash. Always good to have a spare on hand. I threw the leash in the trash at the pet store. It was too dirty to save." The judge looked at Jake and rolled his eyes, a now-familiar gesture on his part.

Aunt Jenny plopped wearily down in a chair. "Oh, my, such a day we've had."

"Let me get you a glass of water." The judge hurried to the cupboard where Susan kept glasses, filled one with ice and then cold water.

"And let me pour you a Scotch," Jake said to the older man.

Susan got herself a glass of wine and when they were all settled around the table, she asked, "Why was it such a day?" A quick look from the judge told her that was the wrong question.

"We went to that big pet store, whatever it's called, and Lucy had her first lesson. See how well she does on the leash?" Lucy, by now apparently also exhausted by her day, was lying at Aunt Jenny's feet.

Jake got the dog a bowl of water, which she lapped gratefully.

"She must be a fast learner," Susan said, trying hard to be encouraging. "Did they say how old she is?"

"About four months, as I thought," the judge said with a sigh. "She's got a lot of growing to do." He looked resigned.

Jake said the last thing Susan wanted to hear him say. "Judge, I envy you. I may steal that dog. I've wanted one for a long time, a big dog like she's going to be. She's a real beauty."

Aunt Jenny sat up indignantly, all her spark back, "Jake Phillips, you may not have her. Neither can John. She's my dog."

"Yes, ma'am," Jake muttered.

"So what was wrong with your day?" Susan persisted, in spite of the judge's repeated warning look.

"There were men with guns there." Jenny seemed near apoplexy.

"Where?"

Aunt Jenny favored Susan with a look that she would have given her when she was five years old. "In the pet store. And they had two big dogs. They were cruel-looking men. Both of them had ponytails, disgusting on grown men, and one's face reminded me of a porker my dad kept in the hog pen."

Susan threw Jake a knowing glance, and this time she couldn't hide the smile.

Aunt Jenny wasn't through with the men and their rifles. "They paraded around like they owned the store. Lucy and I were both afraid, and John was no help. I expected him to tell them to get their guns out of that store, but he told me to just ignore them. I was so scared I couldn't forget about them, and poor little Lucy knew I was scared. I took her right out to the car, while John paid for our purchases. I was so thankful those men never looked our way."

Susan knew dogs picked up their owners' emotions, but she doubted Lucy had been with Aunt Jenny long enough nor was old enough to tune in.

The judge drew a deep breath. "I tried to explain to Jenny about open-carry laws, but she didn't want to listen. I was truly afraid she'd accost one of them, and we'd have a nasty scene, one that I'm too old to take on." Shrugging, the judge looked affectionately at Jenny. "Not that I wouldn't leap to her defense."

Jake couldn't help himself. He laughed, and then he refreshed their Scotches.

"Now, John," Aunt Jenny admonished, "you've got to drive us home. Don't drink too much of that stuff."

He hid behind a grin and said obediently, "Yes, ma'am."

"Well, I swear, Susan, how would you feel if you came across a man with a gun in a perfectly ordinary store?"

"I did yesterday, Aunt Jenny. At the supermarket on your edge of town. I think it was the same men, because one looked like a pig. In fact, in my mind, I call him Pigface."

Aunt Jenny's eyes widened in horror, and she picked up the slim Oak Grove newspaper to fan herself. "You did! Here in Oak Grove? What is the world coming to? What did you do?"

Both Jake and the judge were now sending Susan frantic hand signals. She finally picked up and did not tell Aunt Jenny about her fright, let alone that a rifle was found by the body of Gus' brother. Aunt Jenny would read that in the Sunday paper. "I just got my steaks and checked out. Which reminds me—have you eaten?"

"We stopped for smoked turkey sandwiches at the Hard Eight in Stephenville. Most of Jenny's is in a box in the car. She was too upset to eat."

While Jake excused himself to take a phone call, Susan's mind scrambled, trying to figure out how to make two steaks feed four. She and Jenny didn't eat that much meat anyway, and salad and the artichoke should stretch the meal. But Aunt Jenny didn't eat artichokes, didn't like the idea of dipping a leaf in sauce and running it through her teeth. They'd tried that on her before.

The judge was playing with Lucy. Pretend boxing with her, which she seemed to love. Her little jaws would snap, and her paws would bat at his hand. Sometimes she'd yap in that puppy-bark sound. When Jake came back, he looked so envious, Susan had a fleeting premonition that there was a dog in her future.

Jake seemed oblivious to the dinner problem. "You sure you don't want me to keep Lucy? Kind of train her for you?"

Before Jenny could speak, the judge spoke up. "Jake, I'm sure. Jenny would disown us both, and you might not be as happy as you think. She wants to go out two or three times a night."

Susan bit her tongue, not wanting to ask who was sleeping where or where Lucy was sleeping. After all the months she and Jake had tiptoed around to keep Aunt Jenny from knowing that Jake frequently stayed at her house, she thought she'd caught them.

Aunt Jenny pushed herself up from the table with an effort unlike her. "You all show up for Sunday dinner tomorrow. Basil lime chicken—a new recipe I found. We'll be there right after church, won't we, John?"

He held up his hand as if making a solemn vow.

Susan and Jake agreed to be there about twelve-thirty. They all exchanged hugs. As Lucy trailed out the door, she threw loving looks at Jake.

* * * *

Jake voted to refrigerate the steaks and artichoke and go to Subie's Café. Susan was about to protest, after all she'd gone through to get those steaks, but she thought better of it. Jake needed whatever he needed right now, and she'd go along with him.

The closest she got to protest was, "If we don't eat them tomorrow night, we'll have to freeze them. And I hate to freeze good steaks."

He kissed her lightly on the forehead. "Me, too. We'll eat them tomorrow. I need chicken-fried steak ... and a little Marge gossip."

Jake told her what he was thinking on the drive to the café. "That was Atwater on the phone a bit ago. He wants to find out what the mood in town is. He's really worried about alienating the townspeople when the university needs them to be proud the school's here in Oak Grove. He likes peace, and apparently, the mayor called him today, concerned that the gun nuts have a connection to the school. Why did we ever elect that idiot?"

"Because he has a lot of friends in town, and they voted for him." Susan knew Jake took it seriously when Doctor Atwater, the provost of the university, called him about a problem.

"Did you?" Jake was incredulous.

"Of course not. But half the faculty doesn't even live in Oak Grove . . . or the staff. You, for instance. Did you vote?"

He slammed his hand on the steering wheel. "I'm too far out in the country, not eligible. I vote in county, state, and national elections. But I wouldn't have voted for that old goat."

Susan knew that the description "old goat" fit Hizzoner Bertram Belton only too well. He was a short man, given to pomposity because of his exalted office. He liked to lace his hands together over his adequate stomach and make meaningless announcements on state occasions—like any time a reporter interviewed him. Belton owned the independent hardware store in town and railed constantly about the big chain store out on the highway. Susan thought more people would shop at Belton's if the mayor weren't so unpleasant about it.

"Marge always puts a bad spin on gossip," she reminded him.

"I know, but let's see what she says."

Subie's Café was down-home, old-fashioned in every sense of the word. Checkered tablecloths, mismatched chairs, ketchup and mustard bottles on the tables. The wood walls were covered with photos, many of them from the university, but there were old-time western movie posters, a prominent picture of Mayor Belton, cowboy hats, ranch brands, and a lot else that spoke to the place's heritage in West Texas.

Marge, pushing sixty and a bit plump with that magenta hair that seemed popular with a few females of all ages, greeted them with, "Haven't seen you two in a long time."

Susan wanted to retort that was because Marge had as much as accused her of murder, and Aunt Jenny was still so mad she wouldn't come back to Subie's. Jenny had gone there once alone and anonymously during the murder investigation, and Marge, in her gossipy way, as much as accused Susan of murder. Aunt Jenny didn't forget easily, but Susan saw no reason to bring all that up again. "We've been cooking at home," she said.

Marge waved her hand and told them to sit anywhere they wanted in the almost-empty restaurant. "Don't suppose you need menus?"

"Nope," Jake said cheerfully. "I'll have a beer, and Susan will have chardonnay."

How does he know? I might have a beer with my cheeseburger tonight. She smiled brightly at Marge.

When Marge delivered the drinks and water, Jake said, "What's new, Marge? What kind of gossip are you hearing?"

"Go on with you, Jake Phillips. You know I don't pay no attention to gossip. But I can tell you folks in this town are upset. Two murders on the campus in one year or at least of students, even if one wasn't actually on campus . . . that's enough to make people lock their doors and never come out of their houses. Heard the mayor say just yesterday it's bad for business, gonna cut down on tourists and the like just when we head into the summer tourist season."

Susan had never been able to figure out why anyone even thought Oak Grove was a tourist destination. Sure, the town had worked hard to attract business owners and renovate the old buildings in its downtown area—if it could be called such. Today those buildings housed boutiques, antique stores, junk stores—no other word for it—a tearoom, and a restaurant with ritzy pretensions. Subie's was a hangover from the old days. But still, it wasn't like Oak Grove was near any scenic attractions, unless you particularly liked cattle or sheep and dusty, barren land.

"I don't think it'll hurt business," Jake assured her, "and the sheriff will have this case solved before you know it."

"Well, then there's all them guys walking around town with rifles over their shoulders. One fellow told me he knew they came here because of all the free-thinkers at the college."

Susan waited for Jake to answer, knowing he was absolutely baffled by how to explain liberals, conservatives, and ultra-right wing in terms Marge would accept and understand.

Finally, he managed, "I think the university is as much opposed to those people carrying rifles as you and I are, Marge. We'd like to see guns banished from streets as much as you would."

Marge backed off quickly. "Oh, I don't think you can take folks' guns away from them. Not in this part of the world. The Second Amendment, you know—we got a right to protect ourselves and, of course, to hunt."

Susan took a large sip of wine, while Jake did an equally quick backstep. "Oh, I didn't mean to take guns away from people. But I don't think people need to carry assault-quality rifles into stores and restaurants. You had any of those guys in here?"

Marge got a kind of dreamy look. "Yeah, we have had. It's a bit troubling, but they put the rifles down to eat. And most of 'em are really nice guys."

Susan was silently calculating Pigface's age. *Could Marge have been flirting with them?*

The cook called from the kitchen, and Marge turned away. In a minute, she plopped their dinners down in front of them, almost splashing Susan with salad dressing. "Y'all enjoy. Holler if you need something." Other customers stood waiting to be seated, and she left Susan and Jake to eat without her gossip. Susan almost breathed an audible sigh of relief but caught herself.

Susan didn't really feel they could talk about guns and Jesse and the university where Marge could overhear them. She ate her cheeseburger with more relish than she expected, and Jake ate his chicken-fried without speaking, apparently enjoying it. Susan thought the conversation would come on the way home.

She was wrong. Talk took a turn she hadn't expected.

Jake always drove with concentration, his eyes on the road ahead, his mind alert for careless drivers, drunk drivers—especially on a Saturday night. Sometimes he didn't talk at all; when he did, he rarely looked at her, and that was the case this night.

Without turning his head, he said, "Susan, if you and I moved in together, I could have a dog."

She hooted. She couldn't help it. "Is that why you want to move in with me? So you can have a dog?"

He flashed a look at her, just long enough for her to see that his eyes were laughing. "Well, it's not your cooking. It could be your body. But, yeah, it's a dog."

"I can hear the conversation now. 'Aunt Jenny, Jake has moved in with me so he can have a dog.' She'd be horrified."

Jake was less jovial now. "I think you underestimate the relationship between the judge and Aunt Jenny. Just because they are elderly doesn't mean they aren't living. Besides, you're missing my point. I don't want to move in with you. I want you to move in with me. My house is much more private, out in the country . . ."

"And arranged just for you, Jake. There's no place for me, my things, my books . . . and I don't want to drive that far every day. Haven't we had this discussion before?"

It was indeed a long debate between them. Susan didn't see how a dog changed the situation at all, except that maybe Jake was using it as an excuse. "Tell you what. We'll house hunt. When we find one that suits both of us, we'll put our houses on the market and see what happens. It's the only fair way."

Jake set his jaw. "Let me think about it."

Susan was not one to give up. "You could design a man-cave like you have now, and we'd gradually redo the kitchen to fit what you want."

"I said I'd think about it," he snapped.

By the time they got to Susan's house, he had other things on his mind. She didn't distract him by reminding that he'd only been to his house to change clothes for a week or more. So much for country living.

* * * *

Jesse Conroy's murder captured the entire front page of the *Oak Grove News* Sunday, and much of it was about his father's indignation. Buster Conroy was quoted saying he'd brought that boy up in God's ways, done the best he could, and he didn't know where Jesse had gone astray. There was no hint of grief or compassion in his comments.

Jesse's high school graduation picture showed a young man with curly hair, eyes sparkling with laughter, mouth twisted in just a slight smile. You could tell by looking that he was a hit with the girls. At the same time, he looked young and vulnerable, and the photo made Susan sad. *How did he end up in a field, dead, with a rifle beside him?* Other than the newspaper article, she and Jake had no idea how the Conroy family was taking the murder.

In truth, Gus Conroy and his parents had been awakened late Friday night by Sheriff Wainwright, who came to tell them the sad news. The next morning, Gus could not erase the image of his father, shaking in righteous anger, denouncing everyone, especially God and Jesse. His mom sat sobbing in a chair at the dining table, her hair disheveled from sleep, her robe hastily pulled on and slightly askew.

Gus himself wasn't sure how to react. He'd figured out by then that Jesse was in trouble, but he didn't expect it to be this bad. He was sad, no doubt about it, but he thought maybe he was mostly sad for his mom and for her grief. After all, Jesse was the baby of the family, and she'd always treated him as such. And Gus was angry at his father, his righteousness, his indignation that this could happen in this family.

When a reporter knocked on the door the next day, Gus expected Buster Conroy to tell him where the hell to go. But instead his father welcomed the nervous young man inside and said, "I'll tell the world I tried to raise that boy right, and I don't know where he went wrong." His words appeared almost verbatim in the Sunday morning paper, and Gus knew that cub reporter had to hustle to get the story in on time.

Next morning, Gus thought about Amanda and thought he should call her. But he was reluctant. Nobody likes to be the bearer of such tidings.

* * * *

If Amanda hadn't made herself go to breakfast Saturday morning at the student union, she wouldn't have known the news. Later, she thought it was one of those moments she wished she could recall, like people recall messages on the internet. That always struck her as silly—the message was already out there. Recalling it didn't erase it from people's memories. And recalling this moment, when she saw the headline in a newspaper carelessly left behind in the booth she slid into, she knew that recalling the moment wouldn't erase the message. Jesse was dead. She didn't even read the article.

She thought about calling Gus, then thought better of it. He would be with his family, and they would be grieving, or so she assumed. Going home to her parents was still out of the question. How could she tell them why Jesse Conroy was so important and what his death meant to her? Her father was about as strict in his views as Jesse's father. No, she had to keep this to herself.

For once in her young life, Amanda wished she'd made girlfriends. She wished now for someone she could talk to, share the pain of her life. She pushed her plate away impatiently, breakfast mostly uneaten because she felt so sick, and hurried back to her room. Once there, she threw herself on her bed, sobbing. Finally, exhausted, she slept.

Amanda's roommate, Jill, came in about four, and Amanda roused herself from her stupor.

"You look like hell," Jill said. "You okay?"

Amanda sat up and ran her hand through her tousled hair. "Sure, just tired. I . . . I guess I didn't realize I fell asleep."

"How long did you sleep?"

Amanda looked at her bedside clock and said, her tone dull, "Since ten-thirty or so." She realized she'd slept over five hours, and suddenly the dam burst. All the emotions she'd been holding back came tumbling out as she cried again, telling Jill about Jesse's death and how she didn't know how she'd survive without him.

Jill, to whom blind devotion was still a mystery, was stunned. "Why?"

Amanda took a deep breath. "Because I loved him." She didn't add that she was carrying his baby.

"Amanda, I told you before he was no good. He would have made your life miserable. Already did. I know he broke up with you. I'm sorry he's dead, but this isn't the end of your life, too."

Had Jesse blabbed about it—or bragged? "How did you know that?"

"I hear things. And I met Jesse at a bar on the edge of town."

"I hated for him to go those places."

Jill sat down next to her roommate. "Amanda, Jesse was a wild boy. You weren't going to tame him."

"I've known him since I was a kid. Had a crush on him since I was five."

Jill was the practical, hard-headed one. "Exactly. A crush. Time to outgrow it. I'm sorry when anybody's dead. But grieve for him, not for what you've lost."

And not for what I'm left with, Amanda thought. Clearly, she wouldn't be confiding in Jill about the pregnancy. It still bothered her that Jill seemed to know something more about Jesse, something she wasn't telling.

"Let's go get pizza," Jill suggested.

Amanda gathered herself and said, "Let me fix my face. And no beer for me."

"Deal."

* * * *

Jake spent Sunday morning on his phone, so Susan struggled with Zane Grey notes until it was time to get dressed for Sunday dinner at Aunt Jenny's. They arrived just as the judge pulled into the driveway.

Aunt Jenny bustled about the kitchen, stopping every once in a while to wring her hands and say, "What a sad, awful business. That poor young man."

Susan didn't dare suggest that the poor young man must have done something to get himself where he ended up. Instead, she asked, "What will you do about contacting Gus?"

Aunt Jenny had her answer ready. "I'll go to the market tomorrow. Funeral's not until Wednesday, so maybe Gus will be working. If it were me, I'd be working to distract myself. If he's not there, I don't know what I'll do." She ran a hand through her hair, further disturbing what was already a disarrayed coiffure.

Basil lime chicken turned out to be a real treat—chicken marinated until it was soft and moist and then grilled and served in a basil-lime sauce that blended flavors perfectly. Served with rice and fresh green beans, it was a great change from pot roast and roast chicken. Jake asked for the recipe.

They all tried to make Sunday dinner a festive event, but it didn't quite work. They were sad and distracted and conversation dulled to "Please pass the tea" or "More, Jake?" Lucy lay disconsolately by their feet.

The doorbell rang just after they got up from the table. The judge went to answer it, and as he swung open the door, he issued a hearty, "Come in this house, son. We've been worried about you."

Gus Conroy made a tentative, hesitant entry, stopping just inside the door. "I . . . am I interrupting anything? You're at dinner, aren't you?" His voice was faint and whispery.

"No, son, we just finished, but if I know Jenny Hogan there's plenty left for you."

"On, no, sir. I . . . well, I couldn't eat."

Lucy heard her savior and came bounding forward to greet Gus. He leaned down to pet her and fondle her ears, and she sat leaning against his leg.

Jake came forward silently and put an arm about the young man's shoulders. "We were talking . . . and worrying about you earlier. You okay?"

"No, sir. I don't know that I'll ever be okay. Me and Jesse, we were close. Least we had been until he went to college. We sort of grew apart. But I can't imagine life without Jesse. He was all the things I'm not—fun, lively, a daredevil, a hit with the girls. I . . . I'm dull and stodgy, not as good-looking as he was, and I've probably had five dates in my whole life." He looked forlorn.

Aunt Jenny rushed forward. "Gus Conroy, don't you talk that way. You have compassion for animals, and nothing says more about what a good person you are."

He mustered a wry grin. "Don't tell my dad that. He's already all het up."

The judge said, "Son, he's hiding his grief about your brother behind all that anger. What we've got to do is figure out why your brother was out in that pasture and who killed him."

Jake cleared his throat and said, "It's Walter Wainwright's case. I'm sure he'll figure it out."

But Gus went on. "I don't want to know those things. If my dad finds out, he'll probably kill that person . . . or me. I don't want to know any more about Jesse."

The judge urged Gus to sit, and when he did, Lucy immediately put her head on his knee. He patted her absently while he talked.

Jake sat down next to Gus. "If you know anything that might help Sheriff Wainwright—who Jake's friends were, what girls he was dating, anything like that—it's important that you talk to the sheriff. Or you can tell me."

Gus shook his head. "Nothing to tell. I just don't want to know any more. Don't want to know what happened to Jesse. He's gone."

Aunt Jenny came forward and inched between Jake and Gus, forcing Jake to move. "How's your mother, Gus?"

"She took to her bed. I haven't seen her since she got the news. I guess she's grieving pretty bad."

"Can I do anything? Bring a pot of soup or something?"

"No, ma'am. I don't think you should do that. Pa wouldn't like it. He . . . he says Jesse brought disgrace on us, and we have to hold our heads up and move on." He paused a minute and then, his voice tentative again, asked, "Miss Hogan? Could you come to the funeral Wednesday? It would mean a lot to me to see you there."

"Of course, I'll be there. I'd been planning on it all along." The white lie came smoothly out of her mouth, and Gus never knew she'd wondered how to comfort Gus and his family.

Susan wondered if her aunt's fingers were crossed, but she decided at that moment to go to the funeral with Aunt Jenny.

Gus left not long after, still politely refusing Aunt Jenny's offers of food.

As soon as he was gone, Jenny went to the freezer and pulled out a hen.

"Jenny Hogan, what are you doing?" Judge Jackson demanded.

"Why, I'm going to simmer this hen all night and take chicken soup to that poor woman tomorrow. I'm not afraid of whatever-his-name Conroy." Then she added, "John, you can drive me there. I don't know where they live, but I bet you do."

His thanks were muttered at best. "There goes my day. We've got to take Lucy to the vet too for a checkup, shots, and see about a chip."

"What chip?" Jenny asked.

John explained about micro-chipping dogs, and Aunt Jenny looked horrified.

"Does it hurt them?"

* * * *

Back at Susan's house after their noon meal, Jake once again seemed glued to his phone. Susan eavesdropped enough to figure out he talked to the provost, Chester Atwater, who wanted him to cooperate in every way with the investigation and keep it as low-key as possible in the news. Jake promised but reminded Atwater that it wasn't his case. Then he talked to Sheriff Wainwright and finally to Dirk Jordan, detective on the Oak Grove police force and Susan's nemesis. Jake took that call out on the deck and closed the door behind him.

She tried eavesdropping through the window but could hear nothing. She considered taking a beer out to him and sitting companionably while he talked, but she knew he'd immediately come in the house. She took the beer out anyway, and he said into the phone, "Hold on a minute," and then waved his thanks to her. It started to get dark and still Jake didn't come in. Susan switched on the porch light, which she considered a gentle hint.

Suppertime came, and she got out the steaks, cooked the artichoke—Jake would have to make the Hollandaise—and started on a salad. On a whim, she made up a salad dressing as she went along. "Two parts oil to one part vinegar or lemon." She used olive oil, lemon, a bit of white wine vinegar, salt, pepper, and, impulsively, a generous dab of anchovy paste.

When Jake finally came in, she knew her first questions was not tactful, to say the least. "What does Jordan have to do with this?"

"Whoa, Susan! I know he's not your favorite person, but he's trying to help . . . and he needs help." He wrinkled his nose. "Do I smell fish?"

"No, just my fishy temper," she snapped. "Tell me what he said."

"Let me start these steaks first—haven't even lit the grill—and get another beer." He made fast work of lighting the grill, seasoning and searing the steaks, and then leaving them to cook through. He'd remove hers a lot sooner than his.

"Susan, you don't have a dog in this fight. Please do something big for me and stay completely out of it. If you happen to find out anything about who Jesse ran around with at school that might be a help. Mind you, I'm not asking you to get involved. But if you happen to hear something . . ."

She wadded up her paper napkin and threw it at him.

Jake went to his house that evening, claiming he needed to get an early start on the day and not do his usual routine of rushing all the way out in the country to shower and dress in the morning and then be back at the office by eight. Susan wasn't sure if that was a result of their earlier conversation or if he really felt pushed.

She sat late at her computer, searching Google for open carry-laws, open-carry demonstrations, and the like. She didn't find it reassuring and went to sleep with a feeling of dread.

That night she dreamt that Jake was shot—not fatally but seriously injured. She woke in a sweat at four in the morning and could not go back to sleep.

Chapter Four

Contrary to most people, Susan Hogan usually loved Mondays. The optimist in her said that the start of a new week meant all kinds of possibilities—her classes would go better, her students would respond more, the world would be in its groove. As she once admitted to Jake, in spite of all her grousing, she loved teaching, and she liked her students. Well, most of them. But this day she knew the campus would be buzzing with gossip about Jesse, and because her relationship with Jake was so public, everyone would expect her to have the inside story. She didn't, and she wouldn't have shared it if she did. She thought Jesse probably didn't deserve to be the subject of gossip, and Gus surely didn't. She was angry with the open-carry people who had also worried her all weekend, robbing her of some of her Monday joy. Then she thought they'd robbed Jesse of much more and was chastened.

She had a fleeting moment of worry about Aunt Jenny's visit to the Conroy home but decided there was nothing she could do about that. And the judge would handle it in his own capable way.

The only bright note she could see was that Jake had authorized her—well, sort of—to find out what she could about Jesse Conroy's life on campus. Students were a lot more likely to talk to her than they were to Jake. It was her kind of sleuthing.

Dumping her books in her office, she went to the faculty lounge for the sludge that they called coffee. Unless you got the first-brewed cup, it had a bitter, been-on-the-warmer-too-long taste to it. Styrofoam cups didn't help, even when she doused the coffee with too much powdered creamer and sugar.

Victoria Gordon, the new hire who taught Renaissance literature and assumed a fake British air, was already there. "Good morning," she said distinctly. "I'm so sorry to hear about the trouble this weekend. I'm sure you were in the middle of it." She was a tiny, compact woman, neatly dressed, every hair in place, fingernails polished. She made Susan feel like a tall oaf.

What Susan really wanted to say was not ladylike, along the lines of "Shove it!" But she smiled and said, "Not really. I spent most of the weekend working on my manuscript."

"Oh, la . . . I won't be eligible for tenure for years, but I've already started to reshape my dissertation into a book manuscript. An aspect of John Donne's poetry that no one has discussed yet."

Susan's thoughts tumbled so that it was difficult for her to frame a civil answer. *John Donne's been done to death* wouldn't do. Neither would *I hate people who are so efficient. I also hate people who say, Oh, la . . ."* Nope. How about *Ernie Westin's been reincarnated in female form?* Susan remembered the former professor of Renaissance literature, her archenemy, with a slight shudder. Finally, she managed, "I guess our subject matter is years and continents apart." *Clever, Susan!*

"Oh, la, yes. I don't see how you tolerate all that stuff about the American West."

"Because it fascinates me," Susan offered.

"It's so . . . so physical!" With that, Victoria sailed out of the office, leaving Susan simmering behind her.

Ellen Peck came in as Susan was brooding over the encounter and still contemplating the cup of coffee. "Good morning, sunshine. The expression on your face brightens my day already." Ellen was not only Susan's colleague, she was her best friend on campus, and she'd stuck by Susan through the awful events following Missy Jackson's murder.

"It's this coffee," Susan muttered. She didn't mention Victoria. She didn't have to.

"And I saw Victoria Gordon sailing out of here like the QE2 on the high seas. That wouldn't have anything to do with it, would it?"

"It might."

Ellen looked around furtively and then muttered, "Come to my office. We'll use my illegal coffeepot. Single cup. Always fresh."

"Keurig?" Susan asked.

"I'm not that rich. But this will do. And I have real cups."

Electrical appliances were not allowed in faculty offices, not even heaters for those frigid days that West Texas can bring in the winter. The electricity bill, the vice-chancellor for finance explained.

Susan followed Ellen and soon sat with a fresh cup of coffee in a ceramic mug, hidden behind a closed office door sporting a "Do Not Disturb" sign.

"Scott would have ripped the sign off and burst through the door," she said, referring to the former department chair.

"Ah, but our new chair is a lady and a good egg."

"Good egg?"

"Good person, bends the rules. Easy to get along with."

They both smiled. John Worthington Scott had made life difficult for them during the Missy Jackson affair, among other things threatening to deny them both tenure. After Susan was exonerated and her tenure review postponed a year, he announced his retirement the next June, then abruptly left at the end of the fall semester, taking with him Ernie Westin, the toad. *Surely Victoria Gordon can't be as bad as Ernie, though she's showing all the signs. Why is life so full of unpleasant people?* Buster Conroy, Jesse's father, came to mind, though she only knew him through hearsay and that newspaper article.

Elizabeth Knudson, the new chair, always encouraged her faculty members and rarely frowned. Her desk was piled as high as Susan's with papers, books, and things she probably couldn't find. And unlike Scott, she taught one class in early American literature. Student gossip said she could make even Thomas Paine interesting, and she had a marvelous sense of humor about everyone from Betsy Ross to Dolly Madison. She ran a tough department with no slack. Department meetings were weekly at noon on Friday, and no one was allowed to miss. She had seen to it that no English classes were taught at that hour, but the meetings were blessedly short with little time for discussion. No one could ramble on and monopolize the time.

Now, Ellen settled in her chair, while Susan squirmed in the student chair. "It's uncomfortable so they won't stay long," Ellen had once said.

But Ellen's interest was exactly where that of all students would be. "Tell me about the weekend. I read yesterday's paper, and I figure you have the inside scoop. Spill."

"I don't really. Jesse Conroy took one class from me in the fall when I was . . . ah, distracted. But my impression was that he was much more interested in having a good time than in studying."

"Yeah, I had him in freshman comp when I taught last summer, and he wasn't exactly a diligent student. So tell me more. I want to be forewarned if you're going to get me in trouble again."

Susan's laugh was forced. She wasn't about to tell Ellen that Jake asked her to snoop. Ellen was a good friend, but she wasn't sharing that. Ellen would want to snoop too. "Of course, I won't get you in trouble. This is the sheriff's case—not Jake's, not Dirk Jordan's."

"I can tell you one big thing," Ellen said. "Amanda Meyer, a sophomore, was either in love with Jesse or had a huge crush on him. I don't know if he was leading her on or not."

"And you know this how?"

"From Amanda herself. She came to me about a paper she'd written, which was so overly sentimental I could barely control my red pencil. We talked about it, and she told me the paper sprang from her deep love for Jesse Conroy. I nearly fell off my chair. Wanted to warn her away but figured that wasn't my place . . . or responsibility."

Susan grabbed a piece off the top of Ellen's scratch pad and wrote "Amanda Meyer."

Ellen said, "Don't drag me into this. I've had enough adventure."

"I'm just going to have a little talk with her. When I find her."

"I didn't tell you this, but she's in my ten o'clock this morning. Really cute but really short, barely five feet. Has coal black hair and the bluest eyes you've ever seen. I always think Black Irish when I look at her."

"Okay. I have a ten o'clock too, but I'll dismiss early so I can be outside your door." Susan sipped her coffee, looked at Ellen's cautious expression, and repeated the whole story of Aunt Jenny, Lucy, and Gus Conroy.

Ellen finally broke in with, "Wow! Small world. I want to go meet Lucy."

"Okay. Maybe not today but soon." After they chatted a bit more, Susan beat a hasty retreat to her own office, carrying another cup of Ellen's coffee. It was far too early to call Aunt Jenny about her chicken-soup mission, so she concentrated on what she'd say to Amanda Meyer after Ellen's ten o'clock. And as an afterthought she made quick notes for her graduate seminar in American lit. Robert Frost—easy peasy. Both boys and girls liked Frost. "Two roads diverged in a wood; I took the one less traveled." Jake would always accuse her of taking the one less traveled.

At ten-fifty, Susan was standing a few feet from the door to Ellen's classroom. She watched the students pour out until she spotted the girl she was sure was Amanda Meyer—she was everything Ellen had described except for one thing. Dark hair, short and petite, but there was no bounce in her step and her face looked haunted. Susan blended into the throng of students a few steps behind Amanda, noticing that the girl walked alone. Her pace was slow, and her posture screamed discouragement.

When the crowd thinned out, Susan moved forward, next to Amanda. "Hi, I'm Susan Hogan. May we talk a minute?"

Amanda looked at her, and then Susan saw the blue eyes Ellen had described, probably the deepest blue she'd even seen. But today they were clouded and had dark circles under them.

"I don't feel like talking to anyone," the girl said bluntly.

"Even about Jesse Conroy?"

Startled, Amanda almost dropped her backpack. Then, with more force than Susan expected, she said, "Especially not about him."

Susan kept her voice gentle. "Amanda, I'm trying to help. I know Jesse's brother"—okay, that was twisting facts a bit— "and he's terribly upset. I want to help him, and I hear you knew Jesse better than some of the others on campus did."

Amanda was leery. "Gus is a nice guy, not like his brother." Her tone turned bitter. "Who told you I knew Jesse better than some other girls did? It wasn't true. He knew lots of girls."

Susan noticed the subtle shift of the conversation to girls who knew Jesse, not just people. "Oh, I've just been nosing around. I teach in the English department."

Amanda fixed her with another direct look. "I know you do. You're the one who was accused of murdering that girl last fall."

"Yeah, I was. I don't want that sort of thing to happen to anyone else. That's why I want to help."

"Does someone think I killed Jesse?" For a moment, fear flashed across Amanda's face.

The thought was so farfetched Susan had to keep from grinning. "No, no. Of course not. But since you apparently knew him well, I thought you might have some ideas."

Amanda had picked up the dropped backpack, and they had walked out of Baker Hall and reached a spot with a lone bench at the edge of the sidewalk. No one else was around, and Susan sat on the bench, motioning for Amanda to join her but half afraid the girl would bolt. She didn't. She sat staring straight ahead, avoiding looking at Susan.

This girl is in a world of hurt, Susan thought. "Did you date Jesse?"

"You might say that. But he dated a lot of girls."

"But you more than others?" Susan felt like a torturer, pushing at this child.

"Once upon a time, but not now. He . . . uh, well the way he said it, he moved on."

Jilted lovers always made good suspects but Susan couldn't see this girl getting Jesse out in a field and shooting him, then leaving the rifle beside him. "When was the last time you talked to him?"

"Two days before he was killed." She paused, bit her lip, and wiped at an escaping tear. "He told me to get a life." And then she ran away.

Susan suspected she ran so she could sob in private, and her heart ached for the broken girl.

* * * *

The Conroy home was located near Susan's house, at the south edge of Oak Grove. The judge drove there unerringly, knowing full well where they were going and hiding his doubts about the advisability of this mission. Jenny's pot of soup sat on the floor of the car, between her feet, in a special carrier she had for covered dishes. He hoped fervently that it didn't splash onto the carpet of his vintage car.

He pulled into the driveway behind a tow truck—Buster Conroy was apparently at home.

"I'll come get the soup pot. Just sit still." He came around the car, opened Jenny's door, and reached down for the handles to the carrier. Holding it with both hands, he offered his elbow to Jenny but then said, "I can't close the door."

She laughed, perhaps too merrily because she was nervous, and said, "I can close a car door, John."

They rang the doorbell and waited so long that the judge asked her to ring it a second time. Finally, the door opened, and a woman's pale face peered at them, blotched with crying and swollen eyes. "This is not a good time," she said, her voice breaking over even those few words.

"I'm Judge John Jackson, Mrs. Conroy, and my good friend here, Miss Jenny Hogan, has brought you a pot of the best chicken soup you'll ever eat. She thought you wouldn't feel like cooking, and like all of us, she's worried about you."

Mrs. Conroy opened the door a bit more. "How kind of you. I . . . well, come in."

"I'll just put this on the stove to keep warm, if you'll show me to the kitchen."

Silently, Ella Conroy led the way to a kitchen with cracked linoleum on the floor, a chrome-and-Formica dining set for four, and cabinets whose doors looked to be plywood. The judge put the pot on a burner on an old-fashioned electric stove with wide coils. Jenny turned it as low as she could and hoped for the best. Then she turned to hug Mrs. Conroy.

Ella melted into the hug as though she longed for physical comfort from another woman. She clung to Jenny, until Jenny pulled back and looked at her. "What else can I do for you?"

"Can you bring Jesse back? He was the light of my life. If you can't do that, nothing. But I thank you for caring. It means more to me than you know."

"I'm acquainted with your other son, Mrs. Conroy. Gus is a fine young man, and I'm sure he's a comfort to you just now."

Just as Ella Conroy was about to say something, her husband burst into the kitchen.

Buster Conroy was not as tall as the judge but much stockier. He wore coveralls and a belligerent expression. His fists were clenched as though ready to punch someone.

"John Jackson, what the hell are you doing here without an invitation?"

The judge was unruffled. "Calm down, Buster. Miss Hogan here brought you some chicken soup, and I drove her out here. Best chicken soup you ever ate, I guarantee you."

"Don't need no charity, and don't need people snooping around here trying to find out what happened to that boy."

"I don't care a fig about what happened to your son, Buster, at least not right now. I'm here to comfort your wife. Have you hugged her? Have you thought about how she's grieving? Or is your anger making you oblivious to the hurt of your family?"

Buster looked at his wife. "Ella, you okay?"

She put a handkerchief to her mouth and nodded her head.

Jenny thought she'd seen beaten-down women before, but she'd never seen anything like Ella Conroy. She turned to John with a helpless look.

"We'll be going now, Buster. You eat some of that soup and be kind to your wife and the son you got left. He's one good person. I know that for a fact."

"He'll probably disgrace me just like Jesse did," Buster Conroy muttered, hooking his thumbs into the pockets of his overalls.

Ella Conroy gasped, and Jenny rushed to hug her again. Then she turned on Buster Conroy. "You are the rudest man I've ever met. Whatever your younger son did, you probably drove him to it. And you better value Gus, because he's one fine young man. You don't treat him right, I'll take him to live with me. You understand me?"

Buster Conroy opened his mouth and closed it several times before he finally said, "Ain't no woman gonna tell me what to do."

"I don't make empty threats," Jenny said. "You treat them both right, or you'll deal with me." Then, turning to the judge, she said, "Let's go, John." She gave Ella one final hug and whispered, "You call me if I can do anything for you." She pressed a slip of paper into Ella's hand on which she'd written her phone number.

Once they were outside and before she could explode in anger, the judge said, "Very clever. You had your phone number all ready to give her."

"Of course, I did," she said, fluffing her hair.

* * * *

Jenny and the judge had just returned from their visit to the Conroys when Susan called to ask about it. Aunt Jenny answered and, flustered, began to ramble on about how rude Buster Conroy was, and how pitiful Ella Conroy was, and no wonder Jesse was driven to kill himself.

Susan refrained from pointing out that it was hard to shoot yourself in the back, and Jesse didn't kill himself.

Before Jenny could say any more, the judge grabbed the phone. "You should have heard your aunt, Susan. She'd have made you proud. She told Conroy in no uncertain terms that we had come to offer comfort, and we'd brought chicken soup because she knew his wife didn't feel like cooking. He muttered something about she could cook if she just would, and Jenny lit into him about being insensitive and not supporting his wife and trying to bully us. He stood there, staring. I guess he didn't believe a little old lady would talk to him that way . . ."

Susan heard Jenny's indignant, "A little old lady?" in the background, but the judge went on.

"Then, hard as she'd lit into him, Jenny changed her tone, put a hand on his arm, and said that she was sincerely sorry for his loss and she knew his bluster was covering great grief. Her final shot was that he had a fine son left and she hoped he would treat that boy with the kindness and respect he deserves. And then Jenny turned and marched out the door, asking me if I was coming. I followed her, but then she stuck her head back in and said, 'Ms. Conroy, I'll come for my pot in a few days.' And we were out of there."

Susan sat trying to visualize the scene. Aunt Jenny never spoke harshly to anyone, so Buster Conroy must have really riled her. John handed the phone back to Jenny.

"I have never been so indignant, Susan. I'm sure my face was red and my blood pressure went up forty points—I wouldn't let John take it when we got home. But Buster Conroy doesn't scare me. I'm going back there in a few days to collect my pot and deliver another pot of soup. Maybe split pea this time."

"Aunt Jenny, I love your split pea soup but not everyone does."

"You're right, dear. Maybe vegetable. Good things are just coming into season now, and fresh vegetables make such wonderful soup. I'll boil a hen for the broth, and you all will have to eat chicken salad." And with that she hung up the phone without waiting for Susan to say a word.

Susan's afternoon class on Robert Frost went well, though her mind was only half on what the students were saying. One bright young man, obviously wanting brownie points, volunteered to lead the discussion of "An Old Man's Winter Night," one of Frost's less well-known poems, and Susan let him do it, half listening to the young man who, instead of leading a discussion, expounded on his own theory of the meaning of the poem. Susan realized she'd have to take over—Frost's poems were rarely as simplistic as they seemed on the surface.

Finally, the ninety minutes passed. She asked each of them to choose one of Frost's poems and write a five-to-eight-page paper on it for the next week. Then she told them there would be no class Wednesday. She didn't tell them she'd be at Jesse Conroy's funeral. Leaving the classroom, she wondered why she let herself in for grading those papers, but she knew they'd be good exercises for the students.

She didn't even look for Ellen before she left campus. Just gathered her books, jumped in her battered Honda Civic, and drove straight home. It was far too early for Jake to be there, and yet she was anxious for his arrival. A sudden thought of Lucy flitted through her brain, and she thought, *Omigosh, I'm not going to end up with a dog, am I?* She knew if she did, it wouldn't be Lucy because Aunt Jenny, two or three days into dog ownership, would never give up Lucy. It was a disquieting thought she wouldn't share with Jake.

It was six-o'clock before Jake arrived, apologetically explaining that he'd gotten caught up in some things and no, they had nothing to do with Jesse Conroy's death. He kissed her quickly and asked, "What did you find out?"

Susan hesitated, got him a beer and wine for herself, and said, "I talked to a girl who is . . . or was . . . in love with Jesse. Her name's Amanda Meyer, and she's . . . well, almost bitter. Sounded to me like he dumped her. Her phrasing was 'He said he was moving on.'"

"Any reason?"

"No. But I have a hunch, Jake. I think she's pregnant."

He choked on his beer, spit some onto the counter, and said, "Aw, come on." Then he carefully wiped up the mess he'd made, sprayed kitchen disinfectant on it, and wiped it up with a muttered, "Sorry."

Susan almost laughed. "I didn't know if you'd believe me or not. I have no proof. She's chubby by nature, but she has dark circles under her eyes, a depressed attitude—just a general downer. Nothing shouted pregnancy—no belly bump, no big boobs, none of what I guess are the usual signs. It just came to me that was part of what made her so distraught. And may have made Jesse leave her. She's clearly grieving."

Jake clamped a hand to his forehead. "Tell me you don't have Aunt Jenny's sixth sense. If it runs in the family, I'm out of here."

She shook her head. "No, it was just an instinct. I'm wondering if she's a town girl or a boarding student, but I wore my welcome out in the housing office and the registrar's office won't tell me a thing."

"What year is she? And how did you find her?"

Susan explained about Ellen and the paper Amanda had written and how she'd waited outside Ellen's class. "She must be at least a sophomore if she's in Ellen's class and, at that, one with good grades."

Jake sighed. "I can't check the grades, but I can check Housing. I'll have to find her. I assume she's the one that called me."

"I don't think so. I think she's only just learned that Jesse is dead. I'm not sure she even knows how or where he died. But we didn't get to that before she ran away."

"Ran away?"

"I think she was about to burst into tears and wanted privacy."

"What else happened today?" He was shaking his head in amazement, probably at the twists and turns this mystery was taking.

She told him about Aunt Jenny's encounter with Buster Conroy, and that made him laugh.

"Good for her. I don't know him except by reputation. But our Jenny can stand up for herself."

"With John as backup," Susan added. "What's for supper?"

"Ah, milady, I got chicken breasts. I'll pound them thin and make piccata for us. You make the salad. We don't need much more . . . except love." And he leered at her.

Susan was laying out dishes and flatware while Jake pounded the chicken breasts with a meat tenderizer, when the doorbell rang.

"Can you get that?" he asked. "My hands are all full of chicken."

Susan opened the door and found herself staring at the bald-headed man she had nicknamed Pigface. This time, to her relief, he didn't have a weapon, and his attitude was almost diffident. If he recognized her, he gave no sign.

"Ma'am, I'm looking for my puppy, and someone said you have a new dog. She's a mix, mostly lab, sort of yellow or ginger in color. Do you have her? I really want to find her."

The same alarm bell that went off in Susan's head must have gone off in Jake's, all the way in the kitchen. He came rapidly to the front door, wiping his hands on paper towels. Once there, he put a protective arm around Susan and said, "My wife and I don't have a dog. What made you think we might have it?"

The man muttered, looked away, and said, "Oh, somebody told me you might. Sorry I bothered you folks. If you see her, please let me know. She's the perfect dog for me." And he turned and left at almost a run. A car waited at the curb, and he jumped in.

Jake was futilely calling, "How will we find you?"

As the car sped away, Susan said, "Jake, that's the man."

"What man?"

"The one who was carrying a rifle in the grocery store and bumped into me."

Jake slammed and locked the door and pulled out his cell phone.

"John? Jake here. Someone just rang the doorbell saying he had lost a lab puppy, thought we had it. Something's wrong, and I want Aunt Jenny to keep that dog out of sight. She can let Lucy out in the back yard, but don't let her walk her or take her any place public. Can't explain, but I have a bad feeling about this."

Apparently, the judge said something, because Jake asked, "Did you take Lucy to the vet today and find out if she's micro-chipped?"

He paused, listened, and then said, "She is? Who's the owner?"

After a minute, he said, "What? You're kidding me!"

He listened again and then said, "Something's going on here, John. You take every care. Maybe you should stay with Jenny and Lucy overnight. You have a gun?"

The answer apparently satisfied him, because he said, "Okay" and hung up. Turning to Susan, he explained, "The chip has a phone number. Disconnected. A lead that goes nowhere."

Chapter Five

"What's going on?" Susan demanded.

Jake sat with his elbows propped on the counter and a look of concentration on his face. "I wish I knew. But I have a bad feeling . . . and it has to do with that dog. Don't suppose Aunt Jenny would let me take Lucy out in the country for safekeeping?"

Susan's response was between a laugh and a snort. "Not a chance, Jake, and you know it. Besides, if you tell Aunt Jenny you have a bad feeling about something, I won't be able to keep from laughing. She's the psychic, not you, not even me. And she adores that dog." She paused a minute. "Did you really encourage the judge to spend the night with her?"

"I didn't specify where he was to sleep." He was a bit defensive. "What would you have done if I hadn't been here? You have no gun, no dog. You need a dog."

Here we go again. "But not a yellow lab puppy. I don't know, Jake, but I'm pretty fast on my feet . . . or with my knee. I took that self-defense class once." She wasn't going to mention that Eric Lindler, Missy Jackson's killer, disabled and nearly killed her because she wasn't fast enough on her feet.

"Not enough," he said as he headed back to the kitchen. He stood, staring off into space for a long while and then suddenly said, "Let's go grocery shopping for supper."

"Jake? Are you losing it? You're in the midst of getting ready to cook chicken."

"Yeah, but I'll stick it in the refrigerator. I want some broccoli and a different white wine to go with it. You coming or not?"

Curious to find out what he was up to, Susan nodded yes, grabbed her purse, and started out the back door. Then instinct made her double-check the lock on the front door. *Is Jake making me paranoid?*

As Jake backed his truck out of the driveway, she checked both sides of the street to be sure no double-parked cars lurked.

"I already checked, Susan. You forget, I'm good at what I do."

"You're good at lots of things," she said demurely.

He flashed a grin at her. "Not now."

"I meant cooking."

"Oh, yeah, sure."

He turned onto the highway, heading toward town instead of toward the market that was closest to Susan's house.

"Where are you going?"

"You'll see." He drove in silence but within minutes they were pulling into the parking lot at the grocery where Aunt Jenny usually shopped.

Inside Jake grabbed a small cart, and Susan could hardly keep from reminding him to use a sanitizer. He headed for the vegetables, picked a small crown of broccoli, and then went to the wine aisle, where he finally muttered, "We have better wine in the fridge. I'll just grab a cheap bottle for cooking."

Susan followed, finally getting an idea why they were in this market. "There's Gus," she said, pointing to the meat counter.

Jake headed straight for the counter, nearly bumping Gus with the cart in his haste. "Gus, you got a minute?"

"Mr. Phillips! What can I do for you?" He wore a fresh polyester shirt, blue tie to match the store's colors, and his badge that said, "Assistant Manager." He looked young . . . and sad.

"Can we talk at one of the tables in your coffee area?"

Gus' look changed to one of alarm. "Sure. Anything wrong? My mom . . ."

"No, no. I just have a question."

The threesome sat at a small round kitchenette-style table in a dismal area shared by two other tables, both empty. Jake and Susan declined the coffee Gus offered. It smelled as bad as the coffee in the English department faculty lounge.

"Gus, where did you get that dog that you gave Aunt Jenny?"

"I told you. She was a stray. I was afraid she wouldn't survive on her own. I hid her in my neighbor's garage." Gus didn't flinch or squirm but answered straightforwardly.

Susan thought he sounded competent and truthful.

Jake apparently didn't agree. "Gus, that dog was no stray. She's got a micro-chip. And she had a leather collar and a leash with a heavy leather loop."

He breathed a sigh, apparently of relief. "You can get her back to her owners? I . . . that would be so good. I'll get Miss Hogan another puppy if she wants. I look out for strays a lot."

"No, the micro-chip didn't help. Leads to a number that's been discontinued. For the time being the dog belongs to Miss Hogan. But something makes me think someone is looking for it . . . and willing to be dangerous to get it."

Gus tried to laugh. "Surely not that little puppy. What could be valuable about her?"

Jake shook his head. "I'm trying to figure that out." He told Gus about the man who had come looking for the puppy, but Gus remained unmoved. "I don't know what that could be about."

"Do you have people open-carrying rifles in here?"

For just a moment, it was apparent that Gus was surprised by Jake's sudden shift in subjects. But then he shrugged. "We've had a few. It's the law, and I can't ask them to leave unless the chain's management makes it policy. Personally, I'm like my dad. I'm opposed to guns. I used to hunt as a teenager, but no more. I don't care if I ever fire another gun of any kind."

Susan hoped Jake noticed that Gus' knuckles were white as he clenched his fists on the table.

Jake rose to leave. "Gus, I just want to tell you one more thing. Miss Jenny Hogan is one of the finest, most trusting women I know, and I personally do not want to see any harm come to her. If you know something that could put her in danger or you think of something, I want you to come tell me promptly."

Gus rose and said, "Of course. I wouldn't want Miss Hogan hurt." Just then, the store's paging system called, "Gus Conroy, Storeroom."

"Gotta go. Thanks for coming by. I'll keep an ear out."

In the truck, Susan said, "He knows something he's not telling."

"Ya' think, Sherlock?" He knew better than to be sarcastic with Susan and was prepared for the blow that landed on the side of his head. It was, Jake thought, a love pat, just a little harder than usual. "Let's go cook that blasted chicken."

The piccata was good. So was the after-dinner lovemaking. But Jake was restless through the night, and Susan heard him call out, "Don't shoot that dog." It frightened her, and she wrapped herself closer to him.

* * * *

Tuesday afternoon Susan met with her women's lit class and then prepared to go home. But Elizabeth Knudson, the new department chair, walked into her office and seated herself comfortably in the student chair, not appearing ruffled at all. When Susan heard what she had to say, she thought Elizabeth should have been beyond ruffled.

"Have you heard from Mr. Phillips this afternoon?"

Wary, Susan sat back down at her desk. "No. I didn't expect to."

"There's a demonstration in town. A sort of tour de force, I gather."

"Who's demonstrating?"

"Those folks with rifles. I hear you encountered a couple of them a few days ago."

Is this woman psychic? If so, I'm done for. I can't handle any more sixth sense in my life, especially when Jake thinks I'm beginning to develop it. "How did you know that?"

"Department chair meeting. The provost was discussing safety in general, and said Chief Phillips had told him about your encounter. I'm not telling you about today's . . . ah, march . . . so you'll rush right down there. In fact, I'd prefer you didn't. But I thought you should know that the city police department has deputized Chief Phillips, and he's down there with them. Usually these events are without incident." She fixed Susan with a level glare. "Are you all right?"

Susan shook her head. "No. I'm scared for Jake. I'm scared for me. For anyone who knew Jesse Conroy." She was so afraid she was going to break down and weep in front of this unemotional woman who had only good intentions.

Doctor Knudson was startled. "Surely this has nothing to do with that poor Conroy boy. It's just unfortunate timing."

"I don't know what has to do with what anymore," Susan said, almost moaning. And suddenly the story of Gus and Lucy and the pig-faced man at her door came tumbling out.

Doctor Knudson listened, her expression almost but not quite impassive. Finally, when Susan ran out of steam, she said, "Oh, my. I didn't realize that any of this was related. And you're right, it probably is. My obligation is to report it to the provost and to the chief of campus police . . . but the latter already knows. You realize I'll have to call the provost. It seems to me a scandal is about to engulf this campus." She put a hand to her head, a dramatic gesture Susan thought totally unlike her, and rose from her chair, her yoga-trained figure slim and upright as ever.

"Susan, please try to stay out of trouble. For my sake. I like you." She put a hand on Susan's arm for a moment and then was gone.

Susan sat stunned. Not go downtown? Of course, that's exactly where she was going. As for the provost, he already knew most of the story but maybe he didn't know about the open-carry people and a possible connection to Jesse's death.

* * * *

Two blocks before Subie's Café a police barricade blocked Main Street. Susan simply turned off, took a back way to Aunt Jenny's, parked in her driveway, and walked two blocks to Main Street without even telling her aunt she was in the driveway.

She got to Main Street just as the protestors were walking by—not a march by any sense of the word but a straggly procession of about seven men and two women, all of them undistinguished looking and in worn jeans, wrinkled shirts, and scuffed boots. Pigface was there and so was the young man she'd seen with him in the grocery last Friday—was it really only that recently? Seemed like a lifetime. Susan was particularly interested in the women. With her feminist streak, she wondered if they were beaten into submission. Did not look much like it. They looked as belligerent as the men, their expressions almost a dare.

Townspeople lined the street, most quietly watching but a few shouting, "Go back where you belong!" "Get out of our town!" Police were placed strategically along the street, though Oak Grove didn't have a large enough force to mount a strong enforcement presence. They watched the marchers cautiously but silently. Susan saw Jake across the street talking to Dirk Jordan, and she ducked a bit, hoping he didn't see her.

Susan could not figure out why these people were in Oak Grove and what, if any, their connection to Lucy the lab was . . . or to Jesse Conroy. If they were here for no good purpose, why did they call attention to themselves by parading down the street? Was theirs just a zealous cause for what they saw as righteousness and a determination to spread it to small towns in West Texas? Susan hoped that was right because perhaps they'd move on to demonstrate in another town and leave Oak Grove in peace. But, somehow, she didn't think so. And she remembered Jake's word about hate fueling the open-carry movement.

Deciding there was nothing more to see, nothing that would clear her mind now that the walkers had passed, she turned to go back to Aunt Jenny's. She'd go in and have a glass of tea. She was less than a quarter of a block away from Main Street when she heard the shot. One lone shot, but there was no mistaking the sound. Heart pounding wildly, she turned and ran back—the one thing Jake would tell her not to do.

The street was now the scene of pandemonium—people yelling, shouting, ducking into shops; the walkers looking confused, the police angry, their weapons at the ready. She saw a figure on the ground, with Dirk Jordan leaning over him, and knew instantly it was Jake. Her bad dream had come true! Susan screamed louder than she ever had in her life.

Chapter Six

Susan began to fight her way through the crowd toward him. No one paid the least attention to her pleas of "Let me through!" She elbowed, kicked, clawed, oblivious of the fact that the people she was angering had rifles. Her face was red with effort, and she could feel her heartbeat pounding in her ears, but she kept on. All she cared about was getting to Jake.

No one noticed her, except Dirk Jordan, who saw her as he straightened from the fallen man and immediately blew his police whistle—who knew they still had those?—and began to push through the crowd toward her. He had more command and more strength and was at her side in a minute. "Susan!" He grabbed her arm and then pushed her in front of him to propel her forward. His deep commands of "Coming through" and "Let us through, please," carried more authority than her voice had.

"It's Jake, isn't it?" she called backward. "How bad?"

He bent to her ear so she could hear over the crowd. "I'm not sure. But it doesn't look good."

They reached the other side of the street and Jake. Dirk stood while Susan knelt beside him and took his hand in hers. His hand was cold, clammy; his face was white, his eyes closed. A blanket covered his body but Susan could see blood seeping through the blanket where it had been tucked around his midsection. Bile rose in her throat, and she thought for a moment she'd be sick, right there on top of Jake. The sirens of an ambulance shocked her enough that she swallowed hard, recovered, and whispered, "Jake?"

"Susan?" It wasn't even a whisper, just a voice so faint she had to strain to hear it and never would have known it was Jake if she wasn't looking at him.

"I love you, Jake Phillips." She whispered it in his ear and felt him squeeze her hand.

Then strong hands pulled her away. "Sorry, Miss. Let us at him." The ambulance drivers.

Dirk Jordan helped her up. "He's what we inelegantly term gut-shot, which is not at all good. They'll probably give him blood on the way to the hospital and then rush him into surgery to stop bleeding. We used our emergency supplies to pack the wound, but as you saw it's not working."

"Will they take him to Fort Worth?" She held firm to the idea that the large hospitals would have better facilities. "I want him to go there."

"Can't waste that much time. They'll take him to the Oak Grove hospital. They're capable, Susan. Very capable." He looked down at his useless arm.

Susan briefly wondered what thoughts were going through his mind about hospitals and traumatic injuries, but her mind was on Jake. "Can I ride in the ambulance with him?"

Jordan shook his head. "No, they'll need to work on him, and you'd get in the way. I'll take you there as soon as we get this under control."

She looked at his face. This man she had thought cold and uncaring had a compassionate look on his face and a protective arm around her. Then, within seconds, he was back to business, barking commands, talking on his walkie-talkie, staring at the crowd that was now beginning to disperse.

She saw a small group of people—all rifle-carriers, now without their rifles—being herded toward a police van. The pig-faced man was one of them, his rifle gone, his hands on his head, and his face contorted with anger. The others, including the two women she'd noted, also had hands on their heads but she saw one of the women cast a fearful glance at Pigface, and most of the others looked cowed rather than belligerent or angry. Susan supposed it made sense. What she wanted to know was, what happened? How did things get out of control? This was supposed to be a peaceful demonstration.

Within minutes—which seemed forever—things were getting back to normal, and Dirk Jordan came to her. "Let's go." He took her arm and guided her to his car, an unmarked police vehicle.

As they drove the short distance, she asked what happened and he shrugged. "We don't know. Best I can figure is that it was an accidental shooting. We think, and this is only conjecture, that one of the women shoved the other one and as she stumbled her rifle went off. Jake happened to be standing in the wrong place at the wrong time."

Susan was appalled at the irony—in the wrong place at the wrong time. Her mind went back to the moment she thought she was going to meet her Maker in a grocery store. Why did the Gods above let such things happen? If Jake had moved a few feet away, if one woman hadn't shoved the other . . . The what-ifs were endless, and she drew her mind away from them. "Why would one woman shove the other woman?"

"One thing we're hoping to find out. They're apparently the only two women in this group. You might think they'd band together for solidarity, but maybe they're rivals for something . . . some man's attention, would be the best guess."

"I didn't see any man there whose attention I'd want," she muttered.

Jordan favored her with a slight grin. They had reached the hospital, and he parked just beyond the ER entrance and said, "Police privilege." Then he got out and with alacrity was around the car to open her door before she could collect herself.

Jordan literally sat her down in the ER waiting room, said, "I'll be back as soon as I can," and swung through doors marked "No entrance."

He can't just leave me here waiting! Not knowing anything. Susan stormed up to the desk and demanded, "What can you tell me about Jake Phillips?"

"One moment please. We haven't gotten full identity on a new patient."

"He is the one that was gut-shot," Susan said, the term sticking in her throat.

The nurse threw her a glance. "Are you his wife?"

The words burst out of Susan's mouth almost without her volition. "I'm his future wife." She wondered, suddenly, if those words were true.

"We can't let you see him, but I can tell you they're preparing to take him upstairs for emergency surgery."

"What do I do?" Susan asked, her voice made demanding again by her absolute dread fear.

"I'm afraid you wait, Ms. . . . ."

"Hogan. Doctor Susan Hogan." She turned away before she had to explain that she was a PhD, not a "real" doctor. Still, sometimes it helped to use the title, and she wasn't above that kind of help.

Susan waited and wondered what to do. First thing, of course, was to call Aunt Jenny and the judge. She dreaded it. As she expected, Aunt Jenny fluttered.

"Oh, my, Susan, how awful. How bad is it? You don't know, do you? Oh, I can't bear it. I can't talk anymore. Here, talk to John."

The judge, cool as always, came on the phone. "What's happened, Susan? I, uh, can't tell from here. Is it serious?"

"Yeah, I'm afraid it is. What Dirk Jordan said to me was Jake's been gut-shot." She kept her control and thought she kept her voice calm.

At the other end of the line she heard, "Oh, my God!" Then a pause. "You want us there?"

Susan hesitated. "I don't know. I could use company, but Aunt Jenny's so upset I think she'd make it worse. Can you call Ellen? Maybe she'd come sit with me."

Silence for a moment, and then the judge said, "I'll call Ellen and ask her to stay with Jenny. Then I'll come to the hospital."

Susan breathed a sigh of relief. Bless him, as usual, he'd thought of the perfect solution. "Thank you." Then she added, "My car's behind yours in the driveway. Key's in the ignition. Just drive it."

Before the judge got to the hospital, Dirk Jordan came back through the swinging doors. "He's on his way to surgery. His vital signs are as good as can be expected, given the blood loss. Susan, he's young and he's strong. Be of good faith."

Susan wasn't so sure about the young part. Jake was just her age, thirty-seven, and they were both aware they were crowding forty when, to their minds, middle age begins.

Suddenly he was holding her hands in both of his and looking straight at her. "We both need Jake to survive, and I think on some level he knows that. If you're a praying person, now's the time." Then the all-business Dirk replaced the caring one. "I've got to go see how we untangle this mess. I'm still wondering what all this open-carry business has to do with that young boy's death." He stood and was about to leave, when he turned back to her and asked, "Will you be all right? There's a surgery waiting room if you want me to take you there."

"No, Judge Jackson is on his way to sit with me. I'll wait here for him."

Jordan frowned, and she remembered his dislike of the judge.

Susan was a bit defensive when she said, "He's family to me."

"Of course," and he turned on his heel and was gone.

What a strange man! I never thought I'd see a soft side of him. I thought he was all about crime and punishment. I wonder if there's a woman in his life who softens him. And then she realized that was an odd speculation, because she did nothing to soften Jake. Indeed, he often tried to soften her.

When the judge arrived, Susan marched back up to the reception desk and asked, trying to moderate her tone, how to get to the surgery waiting room.

"Oh, you just wait right here. We'll notify you when he's out of surgery."

Susan opened her mouth but the judge beat her to it. "My niece will want to talk to the surgeon about the findings, the prognosis. I'm sure you understand."

"Our doctors can only talk to family," the nurse replied stiffly. She was getting impatient with them.

"We are his only family," the judge said. Then he turned to Susan. "Come on," he said, and headed for the elevators. "We can find it."

Knowing herself defeated, the nurse called after them, "Third floor. To your right."

They found the waiting room mercifully empty but not for long. First Melba, the evening dispatcher, wandered in, hair barely combed, clothes thrown on hastily, eye rimmed with red.

"Susan, is it true? Is he dying?"

Caught off guard, Susan said sternly, "No, Melba, he's not dying. He's in surgery. Someone shot him accidentally at the demonstration."

"Accidentally, my foot," said Seymour, the patrolman, who had come up behind Susan without her being aware of it.

She whirled around. "Thanks for coming, Seymour. Dirk Jordan has called it an accidental shooting. He's questioning some of the protestors right now."

"And the boss?"

"He's in surgery, has been less than an hour, I'd say. No idea how long it will be."

One or two other members of Jake's staff drifted in, until Susan was prompted to ask, half-jokingly, "Who's minding the shop and keeping law and order on campus?"

"Don't worry, Doctor Hogan. We've got it covered. Jake would be furious if we didn't."

More long silences. Susan tried not to watch the wall clock—she had never seen a second hand move more slowly. One hour passed, then two.

A tall, attractive African-American woman came hesitantly into the waiting room. Susan had never seen the woman, but there were no other patients in surgery, no others waiting for news like she was. After looking around at the crowd, the woman made her way straight to Susan. When she was close, she held out a hand in greeting.

"Doctor Hogan? I'm Tish Hornsby, county coroner. I just met Jake the other night when we found that young boy, but I . . . I . . ." She hesitated as though a bit embarrassed. "I wanted to ask how he is and offer you any help I can give."

Susan took the offered hand and rose at the same time. "Call me Susan. Jake mentioned you, said he thought we'd get along well. Thank you for coming here now."

Tish Hornsby was a no-nonsense woman. "Now is not the time to find out if we'd 'get along' or not. I just wanted you to know I care. What can I do for you?"

"Find out who shot Jesse Conroy?" Susan ventured halfseriously.

A broad grin crept across the other woman's face. "I wish I could. Jake knows the results of my findings. I'm afraid they weren't much. We just know that, despite fingerprints, that boy wasn't shot with the rifle beside him."

Susan nodded, not sure if that was helpful at all. "Will you sit down?"

Tish shook her head. "No, you've plenty of company, so I'll go along. But here's my card." She pulled it efficiently from a pocket where she must have had it ready. "Call me if I can help. And I'll come see him once he's out of here."

"He'll be at my house," Susan said and reeled off the address automatically.

"I'll find you," Tish said and turned to leave.

Susan sat back down, wishing she could tell Jake. Instinctively, she thought he was right. She'd like Tish Hornsby.

After about two and a half hours, the swinging door opened and a young man came out, wearing scrubs and pulling a mask down from his face.

Dear God, don't let this be the surgeon. He's far too young. Susan stared at him.

"Family of Jake Phillips?" he asked, heading for Susan.

"Yes?" She jumped to her feet.

"I'm Doctor Randall, a resident. Doctor Bannister sent me out to tell you that the surgery is going well but will probably take at least another hour. The patient . . ."

He has a name! He's Jake Phillips, a real man with an identity, not just "the patient." Susan wanted to cry out in protest, but her throat was already raw from the screaming she'd done earlier.

The young man continued, "He was lucky. No major blood vessels were hit. Bullet perforated the stomach and exited through the right lung and out the back, so we'll have to treat for infection and peritonitis and be on guard for pneumonia. It was a clean, straight shot. We think he'll pull through with remarkably little long-term damage. But he's going to need a lot of care and rest for a while." Susan managed to thank the young doctor, just before she burst into sobs.

John Jackson, sitting in the chair next to her, pulled her back into her seat, put his arm around her, and put her head on his shoulder, stroking her hair gently, saying nothing but letting her sob. The others in the small waiting room looked uncomfortable, staring at their hands, looking at the ceiling, any place but at Susan. Melba said, "Praise God," and began praying.

Dirk Jordan walked into the scene and immediately assumed the worst. "Oh, my God!" he exclaimed. "Is he gone?"

The judge nudged Susan upright and then stood, holding out a hand. "Afternoon, Jordan. No. Matter of fact, he's one lucky young fellow. Bullet missed major arteries and the like. But hit the stomach, lung, and exited out the back. He's going to be an invalid for a while. I'd say a long while."

Jordan sank into a chair. "Thank God," he said, and to Susan's amazement he made the sign of the cross. "What can I do to help?"

Susan managed to pull herself together and stood to greet him, which caused Jordan to bounce out of the chair he'd so recently claimed. "Thank you, Lieutenant Jordan. All any of us can do is wait." She looked around the room. "I thank you all for coming, but feel free to go on now about your day's business. Jake will be okay."

One by one the few people stopped to hold Susan's hand briefly, pat her on the shoulder, and murmur comforting words. Then they left. Only Dirk Jordan and the judge stayed. They seemed to have put their mutual antipathy aside for the moment.

The judge hesitated before he said, "Susan, if you're all right, I best go check on Jenny. She was nearly hysterical."

"Of course. Call and tell me she's okay. Jake's remedy for her hysteria is a bit of diluted bourbon."

The judge's eyebrows shot up, and he muttered, "If I can manage it." Then he hugged her and shook hands again with Jordan, who assured him he'd stay for a while. The older man walked briskly to the elevators.

Chapter Seven

Susan turned to Dirk. "What did you find out?"

"They're still questioning, but one youngish man let slip that both the women think the leader is their man, and they're fierce about it."

Before Susan thought, she asked, "Pigface?"

Jordan gave in to the first laugh of the day. "Good description. His name is .Floyd Pinkston. We're running background checks."

"Pinkston—pigs are pink." Susan thought maybe the stress of the day was running away with her common sense.

"Er, yes," Jordan said. "One of the women deliberately shoved the other. She didn't think about consequences, and we're holding them both. We'll fingerprint the others and let most of them go, depending on background checks. Personally, I think they're just a bunch of misfits who cause trouble to get attention."

"Dirk," she began and then realized she had never called him by his first name. "I mean, Lieutenant . . ."

"Dirk is fine. What is it, Susan?"

"I first saw Pigface, er, Pinkston in the grocery last Friday. He bumped into me with his rifle and was rude about it. I think it was deliberate. I was alarmed but just got out of there quick as I could. But then the other night, he rang my doorbell looking for his puppy. I don't think he recognized me, but Jake came to the door and said we didn't have a dog." She stopped, remembering that Jake had said "my wife and I." Then she realized that Jordan had a puzzled look on his face, as if he were asking, "Where is this story going?"

"The point is, Gus Conroy gave my aunt a pup the same night Jesse Conroy's body was discovered. I don't know there's a connection, don't see how there could be. But I do know that Pinkston didn't go to any other houses on my street. Just mine. Jake thought it was suspicious, but I think Pinkston is the kind of man people instinctively don't trust."

His smile was grim. "I think you're right about the instinctively distrusting part. But I can't see a connection between the rifles, the dogs, and Jesse Conroy. Yet it almost has to be there. None of it makes any sense."

Before she could answer, a doctor came through the swinging doors, pulling off gloves, pulling down his mask. He was older, his face fatigued, his body slumped a bit as though he were tired. "Miss Hogan?" The younger doctor must have given him Susan's name.

Susan rose. "Yes, sir."

"He's out of surgery. It went as well as could be expected, and all kinds of things could have been worse. I expect him to be fine, but I also expect a long recovery."

"It'll be hard to keep him down and quiet," she predicted. "May I see him?"

"Not yet. He'll be in the recovery room probably overnight. I want him watched carefully. Tomorrow he'll move to ICU, and you may visit for ten minutes every two hours. My advice now is to go home and get some rest. You look beat."

She couldn't resist. "So do you, doctor. Thank you for everything you've done for us. Can you give Jake a message?"

The doctor's smile made it to his weary eyes. "He's still really out of it, but I can leave a message with the charge nurse."

"Thanks. Tell him I love him, and I'm ready to negotiate about dogs and other things."

The doctor smiled again. "We get a lot of love messages but this is the first dog one I can remember. I'll see that he's told."

Dirk Jordan spoke briefly with the doctor, thanking him, and then said to Susan, "I seem to remember you don't have your car. May I drive you home?"

"Would you drive me to my Aunt Jenny's? My car's there, and I could use her kind of coddling right now. I bet she's got the soup pot on."

Jordan clamped a hand to his forehead. "I remember her. She'd fight bear for you. And she's the reason Judge Jackson calls you his niece, right?"

"Right." Susan couldn't keep a smile from her lips. "Small world, isn't it?"

"This time, as long as you and I are on the same side, small doesn't bother me. If you were a suspect again, it would." And with that he guided her to the elevators.

"Wait! I have to be sure they have my phone numbers."

"You can't go through those doors. Tell the receptionist downstairs."

Susan sighed. The receptionist wasn't exactly her best friend after the fuss she'd made, but she supposed the woman was duty bound to get the information to the right place. To her relief, a different receptionist was on duty.

Just to be sure, she left her landline, her cell phone, and Aunt Jenny's landline. Aunt Jenny never missed a phone call. Susan thought her aunt expected some wonderful surprise to be on the other end every time the phone rang.

* * * *

Once in Dirk Jordan's car, Susan felt a wave of weariness sweep over her. She began to reconsider her plan to stop at Aunt Jenny's. It was at least midnight, she was sure, and Aunt Jenny would be in bed. She didn't even want to speculate on where the judge was. Walking in on them could be terribly embarrassing for all three. But a glance at her watch told her it was not quite nine o'clock. Her first guess was probably right: Aunt Jenny would be making soup.

Jordan drove competently but slowly, as though giving her time to rest. The area where the demonstration had been was back to normal, except for one small area roped off by crime scene tape. She tried not to look at it—that was where Jake was shot.

At Aunt Jenny's, Jordan walked her to the door but refused to come in. She let herself in, and found Aunt Jenny and John were in the kitchen. Aunt Jenny was stirring a pot of something, and one whiff told Susan it was chicken soup.

"Susan!" Her aunt came hurrying toward her. "I'm just making you soup. I thought it would probably be what you need."

"It is, Aunt Jenny. The good news is that Jake's going to be fine." She almost fell into one of the kitchen chairs.

"Oh, I know that, dear."

"You do? Did you call the hospital?"

"She didn't need to, Susan. She just knows." The judge's voice was wry.

Susan didn't say another word. Aunt Jenny put a bowl of soup in front of her, hot but not so hot she couldn't savor the first spoonful. Between spoons of soup, she said, "Jake's going to be an invalid for some time." She described the damage, the dangers he faced. "I don't know how long he'll be in the hospital, but he'll come to my house to recuperate."

"Nonsense," Jenny said. "He'll come here. I'm here all day, and I make better soup than you do."

"Granted, Aunt Jenny, but you can bring soup to my house. I think he'd rather be there, but I won't let him go to his house. Too far away, and I can't care for him there."

"Jenny . . ." The judge's voice was quiet and soft, but she recognized the tone and message. It was his version of Archie Bunker's, "Stifle, Edith."

Suddenly Susan thought to ask, "Where's Lucy?"

"Oh, she's outside. She loves to romp and play with her toys. About ruined my garden in back."

"It'll come back, Jenny," the judge assured her, "but I think she's been out long enough."

Aunt Jenny went to the back door and called, but no Lucy. "Now where is that bad girl! She always comes when I call her. Inside with people is her favorite place to be." She called again.

Susan and the judge exchanged alarmed looks, and both went to the door. Susan really didn't want to have to go looking for a lost puppy.

When the pup heard the judge's stern call, Lucy came bounding from behind the garage with a look that said, "Did you mean *me?*"

Susan let out an audible sigh of relief while Aunt Jenny scolded the puppy until the judge reminded her that Lucy had already forgotten and wouldn't know what she was being scolded for, even though she looked most attentive.

She glanced at the wall clock. It was nine-thirty and felt like three in the morning. "Aunt Jenny, may I take a nap in your guest room? I honestly think I'm too tired to drive home."

"Of course, dear. Just let me turn back the covers."

"No, no, I'll sleep on top with an afghan."

"Nonsense."

Susan crawled into the covers and fell asleep almost instantly, but not before she recognized the scent of the judge's aftershave on the pillow.

Whether he spent the night or not, she'd never know. But he was gone when she awoke at six-thirty the next morning. Automatically, she reached for her phone to see if the hospital had called and she'd slept through it, but they hadn't.

Aunt Jenny was up and in the kitchen, Lucy twisting around her legs until Susan was afraid her aunt would trip. Aunt Jenny insisted on fixing eggs and bacon for Susan, despite protests that she had to get home to shower, change clothes, and get to the hospital.

As Susan ate, Aunt Jenny reminded her this was the day of Jesse Conroy's funeral.

"Oh, Aunt Jenny, I so meant to go with you, but now I can't. I have to be with Jake. I don't know what good I'll do, but I have to be there."

"I know, Susan. You should be there. John will go with me. Reluctantly, I must say, but he'll go."

Susan, once more, silently blessed Judge John Jackson. "I'll call tonight and you can tell me about it."

"Of course. But don't call too late," her aunt cautioned.

Susan promised. Then she called Ellen, who said she'd take the morning class. The afternoon class had already been given a walk because Susan thought she'd be at Jesse's funeral. After scarfing down the eggs and bacon, she headed for home, giving Aunt Jenny a hasty kiss and a promise to call.

A quick shower, fresh clothes, she brought in the paper and mail from yesterday without looking at them, and was off to the hospital with the forethought to bring work with her since she envisioned long hours of waiting. But she wasn't leaving. Not until she was sure Jake was headed toward recovery.

She got to the hospital about eight-thirty, only to be told that Jake had been transferred to ICU, which she assumed was a step up, and the next visiting hours were at ten. A long hour and a half loomed in front of her. Often in such situations, she would have called Jake, but not today. Maybe she should call Dirk Jordan.

He was abrupt when he answered, and Susan thought maybe this hadn't been that good an idea. But he regulated his tone when she identified herself. It wasn't exactly warm and fuzzy, but it was cordial. "Susan, I want to come to the hospital to talk to Jake."

She held her ground. "He can only have visitors for ten minutes every two hours, and I've got first dibs for today."

Jordan let out a deep breath. "Would they make an exception for a police officer?"

"I doubt it but you can try. Let me call you after I see him at ten."

"Please do," he said, and the phone went dead.

Susan tried to concentrate on her next lecture on an American lit author—Ernest Hemingway. She was always aware that his reputation preceded her into the classroom, and she had to battle stereotyped ideas to get to the truth about the great man who was so eccentric about cats and Key West and who wrote such short sentences. Students always wanted to speculate on why he had killed himself . . . and she didn't have a clue. It made for good discussions.

At ten, with trembling hands, she went to see Jake. He lay as though in a coma. When she took his hand in both of hers and called his name softly, he whispered, "Susan?" His color was better than the day before but he was no more responsive.

A nurse stepped in to say that he was heavily medicated against pain.

"Lieutenant Jordan of the Oak Grove police wants to talk to him."

"He can talk all he wants," she said cynically, "but he won't get straight answers out of this boy today. Maybe tomorrow, maybe not."

Susan sat holding Jake's hand, softly telling him she loved him, telling him about what had happened since the shooting—not much. When the nurse stuck her head inside to announce visiting hours were over, Susan gently kissed Jake on the forehead and left, but not before she felt him squeeze her hand. He was going to be fine, deep down she knew that. Maybe she did have a bit of Aunt Jenny's sixth sense.

Jordan came to the waiting room just before noon. "Don't suppose I could talk you into letting me see him?"

She shook her head. "If I thought it would do any good, I'd let you. But he's totally non-responsive, heavily medicated against pain. You'd not get a sensible word out of him."

Jordan blew out a long, exasperated breath. "I need his account of what happened. We had to let Pinkston go. He has absolutely no felony record. We ran his fingerprints, ran driver's license, everything we know to do, and he's clean. No reason for holding him. No law in this town requiring a permit for a public demonstration–maybe something we should work on."

"What about the women?"

"We're charging them with public endangerment. They'll go before the judge Friday. But this is only Wednesday. We've got time to question them more."

"Is that a misdemeanor?"

"Depends on the judge. Can be a felony or a misdemeanor. Not sure what I'll push for in this case. I need more information, and Jake could really help me."

"Be patient. Surely in the next couple of days." And then she excused herself to visit Jake. He was in the same state, perhaps just a tad more responsive, turning his head toward her when she kissed his cheek, squeezing her hand a bit more. But he didn't talk.

* * * *

That night, Susan felt like she'd been run over by a truck when she got home, surprised to see that it was barely eight o'clock. Once again, she felt like it was midnight. But she remembered her promise to Aunt Jenny.

"How was the funeral?"

"Susan, how are you? You sound awful. And how's Jake?"

"I'm okay, Aunt Jenny. It's just stressful to sit in a waiting room and then go into a cubicle to stare for ten minutes at a man who doesn't wake up, doesn't blink when I call his name. He's zonked on painkillers, but he did squeeze my hand today. That's a good sign. Now tell me about the funeral."

"It was funereal in every sense of the word, Susan. Dismal. Gloomy. I like memorial services to be celebrations of the life of the one who has passed on, but this was gloomy. In the Baptist church. The minister dwelt heavily on the wages of sin, which I thought was terribly inappropriate."

"I suppose the Conroys were there, and Gus."

"Oh yes. In the front row. Mr. Conroy even had on a dark suit. So did Gus. And the mother, she had on black with a black veil that pretty much hid her face, but I could tell she was sobbing quietly during the ceremony. You can tell by the shoulders shaking."

Trust Aunt Jenny! "Was there a reception?"

"Not at all. Just a receiving line. I went through and expressed my condolences. Gus hugged me and whispered he'd call, and Mrs. Conroy held my hand in both of hers and squeezed. But, Susan, it was the saddest funeral I've ever been to." She paused and then remembered.

"Oh, yes, there was a young girl there, sat right up in front with the family, next to Gus."

"Black hair, short, just a bit pudgy but very pretty."

"That's all I could tell from behind, except that she too kept dabbing at her eyes and nose, and at one point Gus reached over and put an arm around her. Is she his girlfriend?"

"No, she was Jesse's girlfriend until he jilted her a couple of days before he died."

A gasp on the other end of the line. "That poor girl. We must help her."

"Not tonight, Aunt Jenny. I'm exhausted. I'll talk to you tomorrow."

Susan Hogan went to bed without brushing her teeth and slept in her clothes. As she drifted off, she remembered her mother's childhood threat that something bad would happen if she didn't brush her teeth. She was too tired to care.

* * * *

Gus fingered the folded paper in his pocket, but didn't pull it out. He knew only too well what it said. Amanda had slipped it into the pocket at the funeral. Amanda sat with the family during the service at his mother's invitation, and Gus sat next to her, a protective arm around her shoulders, because he felt sorry for the heartbroken girl and wanted to help her. Not because he wanted to be drawn into her drama.

But it looked like that was exactly what was happening. Her note asked him to meet her at the meditation fountain on campus at ten that night. Now, he approached the fountain warily. No one was in sight, and he didn't want to be an easy target. He stepped back into the protective shadows of the trees around the fountain.

The next ten minutes seemed like an eternity, but at long last Amanda appeared, softly calling, "Gus?" as she approached one of the benches by the fountain. She sat, hands folded in a gesture of patient waiting.

Stepping from the shadows, he said, "I'm here," and joined her on the bench, the silence around them reassuring him that for the moment he was safe. "What's the matter, Amanda?" Dumb question, he thought immediately.

"You know what's the matter," she said, her voice still soft. "But I have to ask a favor of you."

"Sure. You name it."

She took a deep breath. "I'm carrying Jesse's baby. Will you take me to a doctor in Fort Worth Sunday? I want to make sure this baby has the best care, even before it's born. But I can't go to a doctor here in Oak Grove."

Gus would have liked to be surprised by the news, but he wasn't. It was just something else Jesse had expected someone else to take care of. "Sunday? I don't know of a doctor that keeps Sunday office hours, and even if there was one, you'd need an appointment."

"I've checked all this. There's a walk-in clinic on the southwest side, closest to us. They're open twenty-four/seven."

"You'd take your baby—and yourself—to a doc-in-the-box?" He was thinking of the kindly but knowledgeable Doctor Baines, who had cared for him all his life until the last few years.

"It's my best choice right now. Gus, please don't argue with me. I've thought all this out over and over. I know a lot of people would tell me to end the pregnancy, but I don't want to do that. I can't destroy Jesse's baby."

"It's against the law in Texas anyway . . . or about to be."

"Will you take me?"

"Of course. What time should I pick you up? Your house or your dorm?"

"One o'clock at the dorm," she said without hesitation, and then added, "I haven't been home much lately. My mom has a keen eye for weight gain."

Gus felt a great wave of pity wash over him. Just when a girl should be close to her mother, Amanda was avoiding hers. He didn't suppose Jill was much comfort to Amanda these days. Maybe taking her to Fort Worth was the best he could do right now. Once again, he found himself cleaning up Jesse's mess.

"Let's go. It's getting late." He took her arm to help her up, and just then he heard the whine of a bullet too close to his head for comfort. Gus acted quickly, throwing Amanda on the ground—unyielding paver stones—and then throwing himself on top of her, not landing gently. He rolled both of them under the slim protection of a bench.

"Shhh," he whispered. "Lie very still." His mind was racing. It must be Pinkston, and he must have followed him. That meant he was suspicious of Gus, which was exactly what Gus feared. Would he kill him or was he trying to frighten him?

It seemed that the sun would rise before Gus said it was safe to get up. They'd listened to two men beating bushes and creeping around, calling to each other. "He's not here."

"Where could he be?"

"He ain't sittin' on that bench now—maybe you winged him."

"Good. I want that son-of-a-bitch to know he can't mess with me. I need him for subterfuge"—he used the big word proudly and self-consciously— "but he's got to do what I say."

"Subterfuj?" the other man asked.

The men finally gave up and stomped away. Amanda and Gus heard the sound of an older car being gunned and heading away.

Gus rolled over and stood, so he could bend down and help Amanda up. She was as determined as ever.

"I'm not losing Jesse's baby that way either. What's going on, Gus?"

He was at a loss what to tell her, but he knew he couldn't tell her the truth. She didn't speak on the short drive except to ask, "Did you call 911?"

"What for? I know who it was, they're gone, and we're not hurt."

It was after one in the morning when Gus dropped Amanda off at her dormitory.

* * * *

Susan spent the next two days running between the hospital and the campus. She managed to keep her office hours and teach a class on Thursday, but she was exhausted when she got home. Aunt Jenny called to urge food, a bed at her house, all sorts of care, but Susan needed to be alone with her thoughts. She'd never tell Aunt Jenny, but she was pretty much existing on cold cereal and black coffee. The one night she tried to eat leftover chicken, it almost made her sick, and she decided to stick to cereal.

The breakthrough had come on Thursday—two days after Jake was shot. He was still in ICU, but when she went at ten, he was propped up in bed and awake.

"Susan." His voice lifted a bit, as though he were glad to see her.

"Hi, Jake." She was determined to be casual. "You look a lot better."

He was less enthusiastic. "I am. They tell me I'll go to a private room tomorrow. But I still hurt a lot. They tell me that's to be expected."

She had no words. The Jake she knew never admitted to pain, never indicated a hint of personal feeling while doing his job. She wanted to throw her arms around him and sob, but she was afraid of disturbing him.

Susan went back for four more visits that day, letting Jordan take the two o'clock visit while she taught her class.

Jordan reported that he had a good but unproductive visit with Jake. "He recalls nothing about the shooting," he said in frustration that night to Susan on the phone. "I so want him to recall what he saw minutes before, but I guess it's not going to happen, at least any time soon."

Having been to see Jake for the last time that day, Susan was at home, starting on the Robert Frost papers she'd assigned. To her surprise, the phone rang again about nine. When she said hello, she heard, "Susan Hogan? Sheriff Wainwright here. I hope I'm not disturbing you, but I figured college profs don't go to bed at nine."

"Wish we could," she said. "What can I do for you?"

"I've spent a lot of the day trying to track down who called Jake about the Conroy boy's body, told him exactly where to find it. Who would know that except someone involved in the murder? I talked to Amanda Meyer a long time, but she swears she didn't know Jesse was dead until the newspaper headline the next day. She told me the names of a couple of other girls he'd dated—seemed reluctant to do that, but she did. Dead ends, both of them. Bimbos, but I could have told if they were lying."

Susan was at a loss, and yet the sheriff expected her to come up with answers.

"You got any ideas, no matter how farfetched?" he asked.

She searched the corners of her mind. "I agree. It must have been someone connected to the murders." A long pause. "Have you thought about the women who shot Jake?"

"What connection would they have to Jesse Conroy?" The sheriff sounded puzzled.

"I have no idea. That's just what came out of my mouth. If Gus Conroy had a girlfriend, I'd suggest that, but he doesn't. I know that almost for a fact. Dirk Jordan is holding those two women on charges of public endangerment, so you might easily talk to them."

"Sounds useless to me," the sheriff said, "but I'm desperate. I'll give it a shot. I think there's more than one person who'd want to do Jesse in—from what I hear he was charming but didn't care what destruction he left in his wake. I'd even talk to his daddy, but that wouldn't explain the woman."

"His mother?" Susan asked.

"God, I hope not," Sheriff Wainwright replied and hung up.

Chapter Eight

By Friday, Jake wanted to talk about the shooting, and said he remembered something. He wouldn't tell Susan, said it was police business, but asked her to call Dirk Jordan. Susan was making it a point not to fuss with an invalid, and, besides, she knew she'd hear whatever it was when Jordan got there. He came to the hospital immediately. The three of them sat in the hospital room, Jake propped up in bed, Susan perched on the foot of the bed, and Dirk in a chair, small notebook in hand.

Susan was so vague herself about what happened that day that she was amazed at the clarity of Jake's memory.

"She shot me deliberately," he said.

Jordan sat up straighter. "You sure? We thought she was pushed, and the gun went off accidentally."

"If it went off accidentally, the bullet would have gone in the ground or hit someone's feet. I was probably five yards away, but she pointed it straight at me."

"Didn't she have it over her shoulder?" Susan asked.

"No, I remember noticing her because she was holding it loosely by the stock. All the others had their rifles slung over their shoulders, as they usually do. I had my eye on her, and I guess she knew it."

"Did the other woman push her?"

"I don't think so. The woman raised the rifle, shot, and then stumbled forward. After that, it all went blank, and I went down."

"Describe the woman," Jordan demanded.

"Bleached blonde hair, long around her face, a little pudgy, angry look on her face. She wore jeans and a light jacket. Not much to distinguish her from the others."

"Except," Jordan said, "the other woman has dark hair. I'm holding them both but will probably have to let the other one go with a stern warning. But why would she shoot you deliberately?"

Before Jake could answer, Susan said, "It's got to have something to do with that Pinkston, the one who came to my door looking for his dog. I saw him at the parade."

"Tell me about that," Jordan demanded.

Jake couldn't add much to what Susan said about the night the man knocked on the door, but Jordan realized they were talking about the man everyone thought was the leaders of the protest people.

"We ran his fingerprints and a background check and came up empty. If he'd had a felony conviction, I'd have had him because it's against the law for convicted felons to carry any kind of gun. But no such luck. He claims they're a peaceful movement, trying to educate the public."

"How did he explain my getting shot? Just curious." Jake raised an eyebrow and pulled himself upright in the bed.

"Said what we thought—it was an accident. He'd 'discipline' the offender. Told him no need. We'd do that, with a jail sentence. That didn't set well with him."

"Let's go back to the shooter. I don't suppose you did blood work on any of the ones you arrested."

Jordan did not like being second-guessed. "No need," he said crisply.

"Did the woman seem in full control of herself? You know coherent, good balance, all that stuff?"

Susan saw where he was headed and almost gasped.

Jordan was stiff again. "They were all a bit spacey. Except the Pinkston fellow. He was clearly in command, and I had the feeling he was . . . angry in large part, but also disappointed that his troops had let him down. The women were vague, responded in monosyllables. Background checks didn't turn up anything, but I don't know how deep the check went. They appeared to be in their thirties and sort of disinterested in the world around them." He paused a minute and then said, "I see where you're going, and I'm having second thoughts. But I didn't smell pot, if that's what you're asking."

Jake shook his head. "I don't know what I'm asking."

Jordan sat back, crossed one leg over the other, and said, "Let's play 'I suppose.' Suppose they're really a drug ring, maybe a way station for drugs from Mexico. Why would they come to a small university town and make themselves so obvious by sporting rifles and advocating open-carry of all weapons?"

Jake thought. "Maybe only because it's so obvious that it would throw everyone off track. Where do they live? Together? Separately?"

"They gave addresses all over town, and we checked. They've rented rooms in various houses that usually cater to students. Landlords mostly said they don't see much of them."

"Possible they have a meeting place hidden somewhere out in the country. But unless you follow one of them, you'll never know." Jake appeared to be thinking as he talked.

"It's pretty hard to follow someone in a town this small," Jordan said. "Believe me, I've tried, and I know. But we've come up with some leads I can follow up on."

He stood to leave, but Susan, who'd remained quiet almost during the entire conversation, suddenly said, "If I were Nancy Drew, I'd call this 'The Mystery of the Women.'"

Startled, Jordan looked at her and sat back down.

"First, there's Amanda Meyer, who obviously knows more than she's telling."

"Who's Amanda Meyer?" Jordan asked harshly.

"Jesse Conroy's girlfriend—or ex-girlfriend. He jilted her. Is this a privileged conversation?"

Jordan crossed his heart solemnly, and Susan almost giggled.

"She's pregnant but she hasn't told anyone yet. She professes to hate Jesse, but I think she's heartbroken. He broke up with her, knowing she was pregnant with his child, just before he died."

"Swell fellow," Jake said.

Susan ignored him. "And then there's the woman or girl who called Jake and told him where to find Jesse's body. I'd bet money it wasn't Amanda, so who was it?"

Jordan was watching her intently.

"And now there's this woman who shot Jake. What possible motive could she have for that? Feeling devilish is one thing; shooting a man in the belly is totally another. It's probably just the opposite of what Pinkston wanted, because it draws so much attention to them. So why did she do it? She claims she tripped, but from what Jake tells us, that's not true. The women hold the key to all this."

"But they're two different things," Jordan protested. "Jesse Conroy's murder is one case; the woman who shot Jake is another."

"They're related," Susan said with assurance. "Trust me, they are."

Jake moaned. "Is Aunt Jenny channeling you?"

"If you weren't in that bed . . ." Susan said and stopped short.

"You'd what? Might be interesting." Jake was grinning.

"I think I'd better leave now," Dirk Jordan said. "I'll get back to you."

And just then the nurse came in to say Susan and Jordan had both overstayed their welcome.

As Susan leaned over to kiss Jake, he said, "Something's bothering me. Something I can't remember. It's rattling around in the back of my brain. But I can't call it forward."

Disquieted, Susan bade him goodnight and left.

* * * *

It was dark by the time Susan pulled into her driveway, and she wished she'd thought to leave porch lights on. She never parked in the garage—it was full of all those things she didn't know what to do with and, besides, how much could weather hurt a battered old Honda? No one would steal it, that was for sure.

But as she pulled her backpack out of the passenger seat and got out of the car, the hair on the back of her neck prickled. That uneasy feeling—*someone is watching me.* Susan lived on a quiet street on the outskirts of Oak Grove; her neighbors were not close physically. If someone attacked her, she had almost no defense. Sure, there was that Mace canister on her key ring but it had been there for four years and was probably out of whatever juice it needed.

Maybe, she thought, she should revisit Jake's idea of hand-gun training.

She fished out her iPhone and turned on the flashlight—better than nothing. Then, making a determined effort to walk boldly and self-confidently, she strode down the driveway, up the stairs onto the deck, and with some fumbling in the dark unlocked the sliding glass doors. Immediately, she reached inside and flicked on the yard and deck lights. Then she retreated, closing the door behind her, locking it, and wishing for a drape. She'd always enjoyed the view of her yard and seldom felt the need for privacy. Tonight, she felt it strongly.

Turning on lamps as she went, she made her way to the front door and turned on the porch light, peering through the small high window in the door. Nothing.

And you heard nothing outside, Susan Hogan. There were no cars anywhere on the street. You're letting your imagination get away with you. Still, when she realized the mail was still in the box on the front porch, she didn't open the door. She'd get it tomorrow.

Normally, if she felt spooked like this, she'd call Jake. Just hearing his voice was reassurance enough. But she wouldn't do that this night, wouldn't interrupt his sleep—she hoped he was sleeping—and wouldn't dump more worry on him.

But when the phone rang, she jumped for it and answered breathlessly, "Jake?"

"Oh, my, no, dear. It's Aunt Jenny. I just wanted to ask how Jake is. And you? We haven't seen much of you this week."

"I've been at the hospital, Aunt Jenny, with Jake." She carried the phone into the living room and sank into a chair. "He's doing much better tonight. I've got to start thinking about bringing him home."

"Well, I told you I think he should come here. I know how to care for recovering invalids."

"He's coming here," Susan said with determination. "You can bring all the soup you want."

"Oh, soup reminds me. John and I took a pot of vegetable soup to Mrs. Conroy today. She seemed grateful, and we talked some. I'm worried about that lady. I think she's hanging on to life by a slim thread and getting no support from that loud husband of hers." Aunt Jenny paused. "I think I'll have to go grocery shopping tomorrow."

That meant she was going to talk to Gus, and Susan also imagined it meant he hadn't called since the funeral. "You do that. I'm going to bed, Aunt Jenny."

This night, Susan took a long, hot shower, brushed her teeth, cleaned her face, and pulled a clean nightgown over her head. Then she made the rounds of the house, checking doors and windows. But the sense of uneasiness had left her. If someone had been watching, he or she was not there now.

She planned to lie in bed and think about plans for bringing Jake home. Instead, her over-riding thought was that several people weren't telling all they knew. There were too many people involved in these two incidents. A probably didn't know what B did, and B didn't know what C did. And she and Dirk Jordan didn't know any of it. She'd call the sheriff in the morning about Amanda.

Jake called at three in the morning, waking her out of a sound sleep. "I remember what I've been trying to think of." His voice was triumphant.

Groggily, Susan wondered if it wouldn't wait until morning, but then she remembered that time was all out of kilter when you're in the hospital. The best she could do was an encouraging grunt.

Jake wasn't deterred. "The woman who shot me—a block or so back in that parade, if that's what it was, she said something to me. I don't remember what it was, but it was ugly. She didn't shout. She was right next to me, and she said it in a conversational tone."

Susan wanted to say, "And so?" but she remained silent.

"She's the one, Susan, the one who called and told me where to find Jesse's body."

"Jake, that's huge. Why would she call you, even anonymously?"

"I have to figure that out, but I suspect it was a way of showing off for Pinkston."

You've got to tell Jordan right away."

"What? And wake him in the middle of the night? No way, Susan. Besides, Sheriff Wainwright is the one I should tell."

"Tell them both," she said. Sleep was ruined for her for the rest of the night.

* * * *

Sheriff Wainwright obviously hadn't heard Jake's news when Susan called him first thing the next morning. She didn't blurt it out, but asked her questions about Amanda. The sheriff wasn't exactly used to being questioned. "Yes, yes, Doctor Hogan. I know I called you earlier. But what is it you want now?"

"I want to know about your interview with Amanda Meyer. I think she may know something important that she hasn't told us."

"And you're calling on behalf of who?"

Susan nearly yelled into the phone. *Listen, old man, you called me first and were glad to get what I knew, so don't turn tables on me now.* Instead, she said smoothly, "I'm trying to help Jake since he's still in the hospital. He's never talked to Amanda, though I have. But I hope you got more out of her."

The sheriff hesitated a moment. "No, no, I don't think I did. My impression is that she really thinks she was in love with Jesse Conroy. She's grieving."

"Did she mention she's carrying his baby?"

"No. And I didn't feel it was my place to ask."

And it's not my place to tell, Susan thought.

Clearly, the sheriff learned no more than she had, but Susan had the distinct feeling that he didn't push. Amanda played the "poor little me" card, and he let her get away with it.

"Did you ask about her roommate?"

"No. I didn't. I didn't know the roommate had anything to do with this. Do you know something you're not telling me?" His voice grew suspicious.

You're getting suspicious of the wrong person. Susan kept her calm. "No, I just thought . . . well, you know, roommates are usually close and confide in each other." Mentally, she was making a note to track down Jill whatever-her-name-was and talk to her. Aloud she said, "You don't think Amanda had anything to do with Jesse Conroy's death?"

"No, I don't. She's a sweet, sad young woman. I've got some other leads I'm following. Thank you for your time." And he clicked off.

Jake would definitely get to tell the sheriff about the gun-toting blonde and the phone call. Susan had had it with this particular law enforcement officer.

She sat and fumed. She hadn't been to the hospital yet, and she had a ten o'clock class to teach. At least Jake was in a private room now, and she could see him on a more flexible schedule. Her ten o'clock class, moving from literature of the East to the Midwest, seemed to last forever, though she thought she did a good job with her lecture on Ole Rolvaag, E. W. Howe, and Hamlin Garland.

One young man raised his hand and asked, "Doctor Hogan, this is pretty grim stuff. Why would anyone read it?"

What a day to be asked that question. He was right—it was grim. "For the realism, for the clear and true picture of what life was like in that time and place. And, sometimes, for the quality of the prose," she said. "I'm not sure you're supposed to like it, but you are supposed to understand where it fits into the development of American literature of the nineteenth century." *There! A perfect question for the semester final!* "Does that help?"

"Sort of," he said.

"Look at how the literature parallels the history of the United States. Maybe read some about what life was like in the Midwest in the mid- and late-nineteenth century. Some of you may want to think about that as a research project."

Feeling rather proud of her answers, she dismissed the class, intending to rush to the hospital for lunch with Jake before her afternoon graduate seminar. Instead, she found Elizabeth Knudson waiting outside her office.

Susan unlocked the door and automatically invited the department chair in. Without an invitation, Doctor Knudson took the vacant student chair while Susan dumped her books on her desk.

"Doctor Knudson, is something on your mind?"

"You might say that, though I'm not sure about it. And please call me Elizabeth, Susan."

A muttered, "Yes, ma'am."

"Susan, how much time have you missed—classroom and office hours—since Jake was shot?"

Susan paused to think. She'd missed two undergraduate classes and only one graduate. Ellen had covered the two classes and she had given the graduates a walk to work on their papers. As for office hours, she'd missed only a few, and she'd made sure her students knew how to contact her any time. She told as much to her boss.

Elizabeth shifted uncomfortably in her chair. "Victoria Gordon has brought it to my attention that you've been gone a lot. I know Jake was seriously injured and that's taken a lot of your time, but I just thought I'd check."

Susan sat down suddenly and hard in her office chair. "Yes, I haven't been in the department as much as usual, but Jake was in ICU and I had to be there. He's in a private room now, so I can be more flexible about when I visit him. But with Ellen's help, I've kept my classes going and my students informed. I don't think a one of them has complained. Have they?"

"No, no. Only Victoria, and I think it's professional jealousy, but I had to mention it to you. Also, I'm aware that you're a bit involved in the search for Jesse Conroy's killer and the reason that Jake was shot. Is that taking too much of your time?"

Susan pondered and finally said, "I wish that it were, but I have nowhere to go with any of it. Jake asked me to nose around campus and find out about who Jesse hung out with and the like. So far, beyond the girlfriend he just dumped, I've come up empty."

Elisabeth nodded sympathetically.

"As for who shot Jake, we know that now or think we do. One of the two women marchers. We just don't know why, but it looks like she did it deliberately. I promise you, Doctor Knu . . . Elizabeth . . . I won't neglect my professional duties, but I will keep digging into these things. I owe Jake . . . and now I owe Jesse's girlfriend and his brother. They're friends of mine."

"That's all I needed to know, Susan. Thank you." As she rose to go, Elizabeth Knudson said over her shoulder, "Victoria is a bit of a spoiled diva, a troublemaker."

She left Susan sitting with her mouth open in amazement.

Chapter Nine

After her afternoon seminar, Susan set off to find Amanda—and if possible, her roommate Jill. Something about Jill nagged in the back of Susan's mind—she thought the girl knew more about Jesse than she was telling. She wasn't exactly sure how she'd find Amanda, let alone Jill, whom she'd never laid eyes on. She couldn't count on help from the housing office, since she'd worn out her welcome there when Missy Jackson was killed.

With a sudden thought, she called Jake. He was alert enough these days that he could help her.

He answered with, "Hi, Susan. When are you coming by?"

"In a bit. But you know you asked me to find out about Jesse's friends? Well, I'm trying to do that, but I need your help. Could you call Housing and find out what dorm and room Amanda Meyer and her roommate live in?"

"Susan, I don't know that this is a good idea . . ."

"Do you want to find out who killed Jesse?"

He was silent so long she thought maybe he'd fallen back to sleep. But finally, slowly, he said. "Oh, all right. Of course, I do. But, Susan, if this backfires . . ."

"Trust me."

"Yeah," he said, "where have I heard that before? Give me a couple of minutes to explain to them that I'm doing an investigation from a hospital bed. Likely story."

"Of course, it's a likely story," Susan said and hung up.

Jake called back within five minutes with the dorm name and the girls' room number. #306 Oak Hall.

"Okay. Soon as I talk to the girls, I'll be there. In time for supper."

"Supper," he muttered. "This hospital food is killing me. Can you bring me something decent? Like chicken-fried steak."

Good sign that he's hungry, but she wasn't about to violate hospital rules. "Every time I've been there, it's seemed like a generous tray," she said righteously.

"But you haven't tasted it. Mashed potatoes without salt and pepper, roast beef with no taste."

"Maybe I could bring salt and pepper." Susan didn't mean to be smart, but it did strike her as funny. She could see all kinds of reasons chicken-fried steak was not good for Jake.

"Susan, go do what you have to do and then bring me some food." His voice came as close to a growl as she'd heard in days, and she rejoiced.

But then she set off for Oak Hall. Amanda wasn't in her room, but Susan's knock was answered by a slim young girl with long, straight blonde hair.

"You must be Jill."

"And you're Doctor Hogan. I recognize you from newspaper pictures." She did not invite Susan in, nor did she look particularly cordial. "Amanda told me you've been stalking her. She's not here."

Susan was so taken aback, she stammered. "S-s-stalking?"

Jill waited.

"I wanted to talk to her and waited for her after class one day." By now she'd gathered herself. "That's hardly stalking. Besides, I wanted to talk to you."

Jill still blocked the doorway with her tall, thin body. She was the opposite of Amanda—lean and wiry as though she worked out every day, with straight hair that lay perfectly flat around her face. "I don't talk about my friends to strangers."

Susan shifted her weight to the other foot, thinking fast. "What if I told you I didn't want to talk about Amanda? I want to talk about Jesse Conroy."

Her lip curled. "Scum. But he's dead, so it doesn't matter."

"I think it matters to a lot of people—Amanda, for one."

Jill relaxed her posture a bit and leaned against the doorframe. "I told her he was no good, and she should move on, but she wouldn't listen. I didn't tell her he kept hitting on me. No way I'd go out with him."

Now that she'd loosened the girl's tongue—or thought she had—, Susan pressed her luck. "Where is Amanda now?"

Jill shrugged. "I really don't know. Maybe she went home. She'll have to tell her folks about the baby sooner or later, and her father's going to have a shit fit. If he'd known before Jesse was killed, he'd have shot him himself." She paused a minute. "I've said too much. I really have to study now."

And the door closed in Susan's face. *Did Jill just let a bit of information slip or did she assume Susan already guessed about Amanda's pregnancy?*

* * * *

Susan realized she'd skipped lunch and decided she had time for a hamburger before going to see Jake. She called an order in to Subie's, hoping to get in and out in a hurry without having to put up with Marge's gossip. To her surprise, the judge's car was parked next to the vacant spot where she pulled in. She'd have to talk to the judge and Aunt Jenny, for politeness' sake, even though she was anxious to get to Jake.

As she walked in the door, Marge said, "Well, it's a family party. Want to eat here instead of taking it to go?"

"If it's ready. I'm in a hurry. I've got to get to Jake by the time they serve him dinner." She rushed to hug Aunt Jenny and the judge, who rose like the gentleman he was. "Sit for a glass of wine, Susan."

Marge had already set a glass of wine in front of her and reappeared with her hamburger almost immediately. Susan dug in, until Aunt Jenny said, "Don't eat so fast, dear. It will ruin your digestion."

Marge had bustled away to take care of customers, so the judge whispered conspiratorially, "Marge was just telling us some man was in here asking about his lost dog. Yellow Labrador pup. I had to kick Jenny under the table." He reached over and took the older woman's hand as though by way of apology.

"He didn't kick too hard," Jenny said, "and I already knew there was something fishy about Lucy—oh, that sounds funny. Not fishy, but you know what I mean. Not fishy really."

She giggled, and the judge smiled at her, enchanted as always.

Susan pressed. "Did she describe the man?"

Just then Marge sailed over, "Everything okay here?"

The judge assured her everything was fine, and Marge left reluctantly, as though she wanted to linger and eavesdrop.

"Funny thing. She said his eyes looked like a pig. Isn't that the man you saw in the grocery?"

"And the one who came to my door looking for his dog. I think Lucy is central to this. I told Dirk Jordan we should call this 'The Mystery of the Women' because they're so many involved—Amanda, the one who called to alert Jake to Jesse's body, the one who shot Jake. And now Lucy. Then again, maybe it should be 'The Mystery of the Dog.'"

"Just so you don't add yourself to that list of women, Susan dear," her aunt said.

"I won't," Susan promised.

And the judge patted Aunt Jenny's hand. "We don't want to add you either, my dear."

Jenny Hogan blushed and then leaned over to kiss him on the cheek.

Susan pushed away her half-finished hamburger and left soon after that, assuring the older people she'd talk to them that evening.

Jake wasn't in a much better mood. "I'm tired of lying here," he complained. "Things are piling up on my desk, let alone Jesse's murder. I've got too much to do to lie in bed."

"Did you walk today?"

"Yes, Mother. Three times. Sat in the chair a lot of the day. Do you know what crap is on daytime TV?"

Susan laughed. "As a matter of fact, I do. Have you dealt with your email?"

"Nobody brought me my laptop." It was almost an accusation.

"I'll do it first thing in the morning. I promise. Or have someone from your office bring it. Any idea when you'll be dismissed?"

"Maybe the weekend. Am I going to your house?" he asked.

"Yes, though Aunt Jenny claims she can take better care of you."

"Probably true. Maybe she'll at least bring homemade soup. The Conroys don't need to get all of it."

"I have a bit of other news," Susan said.

"Amanda?"

"No. I talked to her roommate, but she told me almost nothing except that Jesse kept hitting on her. Then she practically slammed the door in my face. But I ran into Aunt Jenny and the judge . . ." She was careful not to tell him where, and he fortunately didn't ask. Then she had to backtrack and tell a white lie.

"They were at Subie's last night, and Marge said some man was in asking about a puppy—yellow lab. Said it ran away, and he was frantic to get it back. Judge said he had to kick Aunt Jenny to keep her from saying anything, but she said she knew they didn't have the full story about her dog."

"Her dog? She's possessive now."

"From the moment she got Lucy."

"I agree there's something more behind Gus's story about the dog. I've tried to think about it lying here, but I haven't come up with anything."

"One other bit I keep forgetting to tell you. When you were in surgery, Tish Hornsby came to the waiting area. She just wanted to check on you and let me know she was concerned. Seemed like a nice lady. I liked her."

"Good. I hope we'll see more of her."

"She said she'll come visit when you get out of the hospital."

He nodded absently.

She could see he was tiring. "Call me tonight before you go to sleep, and I'll be back in the morning." And she left.

Chapter Ten

Susan had no more walked in the door at home when her phone rang.

"Susan?" It was the judge's voice. "Your aunt's house has been—well, I guess the jargon for it is, it's been tossed. Somebody tore everything up, looking for something. Jenny's almost hysterical, and I need you. I've called Dirk Jordan, much as I hated to."

"I'll be right there." She ran to the car and braked around corners so fast she hoped Dirk Jordan was already there and not watching her. By the time she parked in the driveway, three police cars, lights flashing, were out front.

Susan ran up the steps and then stopped at the open door. The house had indeed been "tossed," furniture thrown around, upholstery ripped, garbage emptied on the floor. Pictures hung crookedly on the wall and the one standing lamp tilted crazily.

Police officers, some in uniform, some in department T-shirts and jeans, worked busily, mostly fingerprinting. Not restoring what damage they could.

Aunt Jenny sat at the kitchen table—in a chair that the judge had apparently set upright. Before her was a glass holding one finger of Jake's best bourbon. She alternately sobbed, stuck her tongue in the brew as if tasting it, and made a face.

"Jenny, take a sip. Dipping your tongue in it won't help." The judge was gentle, but Susan could tell his patience was ebbing.

Dirk Jordan sat in another chair, though when he stood for a minute, Susan could see that the seat cover had been slashed. "Now, Miss Hogan, if you could tell us what time you left today and when you returned, it would be a big help."

Jenny looked deferentially at the judge, who said briskly, "We went for an early supper at Subie's. Left maybe at four, home by five."

"So that's our time frame. Do you usually go out at that time?"

The judge shook his head. "No. Jenny cooks most of our dinners."

"Someone watched to see you leave?"

"I guess so. I didn't notice anything unusual, but then I didn't expect to. Wasn't looking."

"Alarm system?" Dirk asked.

John Jackson sighed. "Yes, but we only set it at night. Who needs an alarm system in the middle of the afternoon?"

"Apparently, Miss Hogan does," Dirk said wryly. If he wondered about the living arrangements, he avoided the topic.

Susan stood on one foot and the other and finally blurted out, "Lucy? Where is she?"

Jenny began sobbing all the louder. "Lucy. I haven't looked for her. John, is she in her crate still? That's where we left her."

He bounded up with amazing energy for a man his age, dashed into the bedroom, and came back carrying Lucy's collar. "No, she's not. But her collar was on the floor by the crate, and someone pulled all her bedding out of the crate."

Jenny began to sob. "They've stolen Lucy. That's what they came here for." Her face went down into her hands, and she sobbed again.

"Jenny, let me look outside." John went to the back door, turned on outdoor lights, called the dog, and finally prowled the backyard. Sybil crept out from under Aunt Jenny's bed and settled herself in Jenny's lap, as though offering comfort. Susan thought perhaps the cat was hoping Lucy was really missing.

After several long minutes, he came back, carrying the now-gangly-and-heavy puppy in his arms. "She was hiding behind her doghouse. Something terrified her. She's trembling."

Jenny reached out her arms and cradled the dog in her lap, displacing the indignant cat. Then Jenny began to croon to Lucy, who did soon calm down and eventually licked her mistress in the face as if to say, "I'm so glad you came home and found me."

Susan reached down and set yet another kitchen chair upright, sat in it, and said directly to Dirk Jordan, "I told you the dog was part of it. We just have to find out how."

Dirk scowled and changed the subject. "Anything missing that you can tell?"

"Not as far as I can tell," the judge said. "We leave no money in the house, and Jenny's jewelry has been pawed through—as have all her drawers. But there's not a lot valuable here"—he shot Aunt Jenny an apologetic look— "and nothing seems to be missing."

"Antiques?"

"Didn't have any."

"Electronics?"

The judge almost laughed. "Jenny wouldn't have them, and my laptop is in its place in the guest room. Televisions are also in place, thankfully none of them trashed."

Susan had been impatiently tapping her hands on the table until Dirk finally looked at her. "They were looking for something specific, and I think it had to do with Lucy."

Dirk gave her a long stare and said sarcastically, "Thank you, detective."

Just then Aunt Jenny erupted in another loud cry. "Lucy's been hurt. Look here at her neck. There's a red raw place, the fur all gone."

Judge Jackson bent to look and said, "Her collar was ripped off. Some salve will ease the pain. She'll be fine, Jenny."

Jenny hugged the dog all the tighter.

One by one, the police detail reported to Jordan but in the long run the report was discouraging: no fingerprints. Whoever did this—and they suspected more than one person—was professional, wore gloves. Nobody could come up with a motive, except Susan, who kept quiet about her conviction it had to do with Lucy and somehow it had to do with the people who carried rifles and shot Jake.

It was nearly eleven by the time Dirk Jordan dismissed his men and prepared to leave. "Judge, set your alarm, be on the alert, and call me if you see or hear anything suspicious. I'll have a patrol car by every so often, but I think that's locking the barn door too late."

The judge nodded.

Turning to Susan, Dirk asked, "You okay to go home alone?"

"Sure," she nodded, wondering if she really was and remembering her eerie feeling the night before.

After the police left, Susan stayed to drink a cup of green tea with her aunt and the judge, though it was apparent that the judge thought Jenny should be in bed.

"I'll put Lucy's crate right next to the bed," he reassured her.

She shook her head stubbornly. "She'll sleep on the bed."

"Under the covers?" he asked with dismay.

"Well, maybe not." And for the first time that evening, Jenny Hogan's mischievous smile returned.

Susan took her leave, accompanied by a warning to be careful and call and tell them when she was safely home. She assured them she was fine and would call, but she found her nerves on edge as she drove. When she reached her house, she drove right on past for over a block, checking for cars in the street, strange cars in driveways, anything that alarmed her. Nothing. But she still almost ran from the car to the deck and let out a huge sigh of relief when she was inside, the doors locked, the alarm set.

She called Aunt Jenny and the judge to say she was safely home, and then saw that Jake had called and left a message.

"Where are you? I can't go to sleep without telling you goodnight." His tone was plaintive.

Too late to call a hospital. She texted, "I'll tell you in the morning. Not to worry. Sweet dreams. Dream of us together."

To her surprise, he texted right back, "I'll dream of you in one of my oversize T-shirts."

Go to sleep, Jake!

But she didn't sleep soundly, alert to every noise, every creak in the house. She longed for Jake's comforting presence in the bed. Maybe if she had a dog . . .

Chapter Eleven

"It's the dog! You were right." The look on Jake's face was so surprised that he might well have just discovered some new theory of light and space.

Susan had gone to the hospital early the morning after the incident at Aunt Jenny's so she could tell Jake what happened and still make her ten o'clock class. Elizabeth Knudson's words rang in her ears, and she didn't want any more criticism from Victoria Whoever.

Jake threw back the covers and swung his legs over the edge of the bed. "I've got to get out of here. Too much to do, too many people to protect . . . and now a dog."

"Whoa, cowboy! Get back in that bed. You're not leaving until you have the doctor's permission, and then you'll follow his orders about taking it easy and so on."

"Yeah, who says?" His lopsided grin appeared as he said that.

"I say," Susan replied, "and right now I'm stronger than you. So put that in your pipe and smoke it."

He laughed as he swung back into the bed. "Okay, for now. But just you wait. I'll be back stronger than ever."

"Sure, sure. Meantime, your office will have your laptop to you this morning, and you have your cell. Go ahead and call Dirk Jordan, put yourself in the middle of everything, when you should be calmly resting."

Jake gave her a dirty look. "What are you doing the rest of the day?"

"I have classes. Remember me? I have a teaching job at the college, and Victoria Gordon has apparently appointed herself to keep track of my presence in the classroom and in my office. Elizabeth Knudson has no problem with it but she did mention Victoria's 'concerns.'"

"Does she teach Renaissance lit?"

"Yep, just like Ernie. There must be something about that field that makes them pains in the butt. Got to go. Try to rest, and text me what the doctor says."

"If he ever comes in," Jake said glumly.

Susan kissed him and left, looking at her watch. No time to run by Aunt Jenny's until after her American lit class. They had moved from Midwestern lit by now back in time to the books of the American West. Susan felt the semester rushing by and skipped from Midwestern lit, omitting Sandburg and others she thought important, to the American West. Today they'd discuss Andy Adams' *The Log of a Cowboy,* the most authentic trail drive novel—no romanticizing, no glory, just the truth about the drudgery and deadly dangers of the trail. Susan always found it a little boring, but she thought it essential for the class.

They apparently found it boring too, and the hour dragged by, with Susan trying desperately to get them to talk about their preconceived ideas about trail drives, working toward a discussion of the myth of the American West contrasted to the reality. She didn't feel she made progress.

As soon as class was over, she bolted for Aunt Jenny's house, hoping for lunch while she helped with the damage.

Her hopes were dashed when she walked in the door. Nothing was changed—the mess of last night was now the mess of today. And Aunt Jenny slumped on the couch in dejection, with Lucy huddled next to her. Judge Jackson was walking through the house with an efficient-looking but attractive woman of about forty.

"John is talking to the insurance adjuster," Jenny said, with a nod in their direction. "They told us not to move anything until the adjuster came to inspect. So here we sit."

"I can stay and help for a bit when she gives the okay," Susan said. "Any soup in the fridge?"

Jenny shook her head. "It's all frozen. There's chicken and split pea."

"Well, I'll just go defrost. Which one do you want?"

Aunt Jenny shook her head. "I'm not hungry."

Susan stood hands on hips and stared at her aunt. "But you'll eat it. I'm going for split pea." And she marched off to the kitchen, where she used hot water to loosen the frozen soup and then put it into a wet saucepan—so it wouldn't stick—and set it over low heat. Aunt Jenny had taught her a few cooking skills.

Soon the aroma of pea soup filled the small house. Susan felt her stomach rumble. John escorted the adjuster back into the living room and introduced Susan to Mrs. Lyon.

"I smell soup," the judge said. "Will you join us?" He directed that toward Mrs. Lyon.

"Oh, no thank you. I have several other appointments. But I think my notes are complete, and you can go ahead and begin to straighten, call for reupholstering and repair estimates, and get that information back to me."

The judge thanked her, saw her to the door, and then swung back into the room with a hearty, "Let's go eat lunch, Jenny."

"I couldn't. I'm not hungry, and I'm still worried about Lucy. She's so scared."

"Because you're babying her." He almost barked the words. "Leave her alone and she'll be fine. Come on, Susan, let's eat." He strode to the kitchen, and after a few seconds, Susan followed him. Finally, after a long minute, Aunt Jenny came behind them, leaving Lucy on the couch but stealing looks over her shoulder. It took Lucy about two minutes to decide the party was moving into the kitchen and follow.

The soup was simmering. Susan turned it down, got out crackers, poured water, and randomly put paper napkins and soup spoons on the table. Not the kind of service her aunt preferred, but it would do.

The soup was hot, soothing, and delicious. Susan was tempted to go for a second bowl, and then asked, "Aunt Jenny, may I take some of this to Jake tonight?"

Food seemed to have made her aunt brighten, and she answered, "Of course, Susan. I'll get you a microwavable container, so you can heat it at the hospital. When's that boy coming home?"

"I don't know, but I'm hoping soon. He complains all the time about hospital food. Just let me call and make sure they'll let me give it to him."

"And why wouldn't they?" Aunt Jenny demanded. "It's good homemade soup without any junk in it."

Before Susan could call the hospital, Jake called.

"Doctor says for sure I can go home tomorrow." He hesitated. "Does home mean your house?"

Susan bit back a sarcastic retort and said, "Of course it does, Jake. What would you like for your first meal at home?"

His answer was ready. "Aunt Jenny's meatloaf, mashed potatoes, and green bean casserole."

Susan guessed she didn't need to worry about whether he could eat split pea soup. "Okay, you got it. I'll be there later to bring you some homemade soup tonight."

"Terrific."

She disconnected and turned to explain to Aunt Jenny, who wailed, "I don't have the makings for all that!" Still rattled by the break-in, she never thought of going to the grocery.

Susan volunteered. "I have a class, then I'll go to the grocery, bring you what you need—make me a list—and go see Jake."

"Oh, my!" Jenny scurried around, found pencil and paper, and made a list, stopping now and again as though she hadn't made this dinner a thousand times and couldn't remember what went in it.

Susan finally grabbed the list and headed for her afternoon writing seminar, which should let out at four-thirty—plenty of time, she told herself. Jake's dinner wasn't served until five-thirty. She'd make sure no one hogged the discussion and dragged out the seminar.

At four-thirty promptly, she dismissed the small class and dashed to her office, stopping deliberately to wave at Victoria Gordon, who acknowledged the wave with a small nod of the head. Feeling exuberantly happy, Susan dumped her books on her desk, locked the office door, and headed for the grocery nearest Aunt Jenny's house.

She had assembled most of the items in her cart when she looked up from her list and saw Pigface staring at her. Uh, Pinkston—yes, that was his name. He simply stood, one hand on his rifle, looking at her. She dodged around him and finished her shopping with shaking hands. What was it about him and grocery stores? Why did she run into him there?

Checked out, she put the groceries on the front seat of her car and started out of the parking lot. As she looked for oncoming cars in the turn lane, she realized Pigface was driving the battered Plymouth in front of her. Swinging into line, Susan thought idly it would be interesting to follow him. Suddenly, a random thought became reality. Susan couldn't resist, even though she could hear Jake's roar in her mind.

"Susan, what in the hell did you think you were doing?"

When Pigface turned, she hesitated, letting a couple of cars get between them, and then she followed, carefully staying some distance behind, grateful that her Honda, as battered as his Plymouth, was not distinctive and not liable to be noticed.

Pigface headed toward her house, which caused Susan's heart to lurch, but then he kept going on the highway, driving at medium speed. Surely not risking a speed ticket. Now there were no cars between them, and Susan had to hang way back, barely keeping an eye on him.

At one point, he came up behind a truck going much slower, and Susan had to choose quickly whether to be forced right up behind him or turn off briefly. She pulled into a driveway on the right and waited while three cars got between her and her object. Then, afraid she waited too long, she pulled out in time to see Pinkston pass the truck. The next driver was insecure about passing, and Susan chewed on her lip in impatience. Finally, the truck turned off to the right on a farm-to-market road, but she'd lost Pinkston. She couldn't pass the remaining car, because the road turned curvy, but as luck would have it she saw Pigface's car take a left on what she thought was a farm-to-market road. She drove on by sedately, giving him space.

In about a mile, she made a U-turn in a driveway and headed back, hoping there were enough houses on the gravel road to justify her turning into it.

There weren't. Far as she could tell, Pigface turned into a dirt lane with a huge sign warning, "Private Property. Trespassers will be Shot."

Once again, she kept going, looking for a convenient place to turn around and finding none for a good mile. The road was closely bordered by thick growth of underbrush and barbed-wire fences, poorly maintained. Finally, she turned at a wide curve in the road—Jake would have a fit about the danger—and headed back to town.

But as she neared the private property sign, a man on a motorcycle pulled onto the road, headed toward town. Susan stopped abruptly and watched the vanishing figure. Gus Conroy! What was he doing out here at what she supposed was Pigface's hideaway. She'd heard Jake and Dirk speculate that the places the open-carry people rented in town were cover for a central hideaway. This must be it. But Gus Conroy?

Giving Gus plenty of time to get a good start on her, she leisurely drove back and pulled into Aunt Jenny's driveway, only to be met on the front porch by her aunt, who was as irate as she'd ever been when Susan was a misbehaving teenager.

"Susan Hogan, where have you been? I've been worried to death, and John has gone to take Jake his soup, though Jake may not be in a mood to eat it. He's worried too."

Susan was contrite. "I got distracted. I'll call Jake right away and head up there. Here are your groceries." She jumped out, rounded the car, and handed the older woman the bag.

Aunt Jenny was not the least mollified. "You better have a good story. I want to hear it after Jake does." With that, she huffed her way back into the house, carrying the sack of food.

Susan got back in the car and punched one on speed dial. Jake answered immediately, with a growl.

"Susan, where are you? We've all been worried. It doesn't take an hour to go to the store for a short list."

"I'm fine, and I'm on my way. I'll tell you when I get there." A dead sound told her he'd disconnected.

When she got to the hospital, the judge was still there. "I figured this was going to be a good story, and I wanted to hear it," he said, with a twinkle in his eyes.

There was no twinkle in Jake's eyes. "Well?"

She stammered. "How was your soup?"

"Good. You know it was. Now, where were you? Why am I apprehensive?"

"I went for a drive in the country," she began.

Jake cut her off. "Enjoy the scenery?"

"Jake, I found out something important. I found out where the open-carry people's place is, and then I saw Gus Conroy coming out of there. Why would he be with the people who killed his brother?"

Jake stared, while the judge clapped in amazement and muttered, "Good job, Susan."

Jake suddenly thundered, "Good job, my foot, John! I've got to get out of here before this fool woman gets shot. We don't need to both be victims at once. That was a dumb thing to do, Susan."

"She found out something important, didn't she? If I were you, I'd calm down and call Sheriff Wainwright." The judge spoke softly with little hint of rebuke, but his voice mollified Jake.

Jake reached for his phone, punched in the numbers, asked for Wainwright, and then handed the phone to Susan. "Your story, you tell him."

Susan gave him a look of defiance and said, "Afternoon, Sheriff. I have some information that might interest you." And she proceeded to describe her adventure. Wainwright listened, only murmuring, "I see," and "good" from time to time.

Then, abruptly, "Let me talk to Jake." Without a word, Susan handed the phone to Jake, who took it gingerly, as though it might explode in his hands.

Both she and the judge could get the gist of the conversation because Sheriff Wainwright talked loudly. Phrases such as "Put herself in danger" and "Could have squelched our investigation" echoed through the connection.

Susan longed to ask what investigation. But the crowning blow came when she heard the sheriff say something about controlling her. Even Jake looked uncomfortable and said, "Not my job, Sheriff. She did a good thing today, even if it was dangerous and foolish."

She shot a dagger-like look at Jake.

He continued his phone conversation. "If I were out of this bed and able, I'd be out there in the country, checking out what's at the end of the dirt road. Not too far from Donley's place where the boy's body was found, is it?"

Mumbled conversation on the other end, in a suddenly lower voice, and then Jake asked, "When are you going to check it out?" Pause. "Tonight. Okay. Let me know what happens." Sigh. "I'll be right here, but my cell will be on. You don't have to go through the hospital switchboard."

By the time he disconnected, Susan's anger had turned to pure gratefulness and love. She crossed to the bed, planted a huge kiss on Jake's mouth, and said, "Jake Phillips, I love you."

"I hope so," he said, "but it was still a damn fool thing to do."

She didn't care.

Jake had relished the soup and urged Susan to follow the judge to Aunt Jenny's and have some for herself. She opted to stay for a while, asking the judge to suggest Aunt Jenny keep it warm on the stove.

"What's up?" Jake asked.

"I don't know," she said honestly. "I don't feel right about all this—I keep wondering how Gus and maybe Amanda are involved, and what the woman who called about the body has to do with it all. Why did she want Jesse's body discovered? And how did the call come from campus? There's a lot more going on here than an open-carry protest, though that is scary enough. I'm frightened, and I don't like that feeling."

Jake held out his arms, and she wandered into them, sinking her head on his chest and feeling the reassuring warmth. Lord, she'd be glad to have him home.

As if he read her mind, he said, "I'm feeling a lot better. Not good enough to go stalking in the woods at night, but better. I'm sure the doctor will let me come home tomorrow."

She kissed him again, just as a nurse walked into the room. "Now, Doctor Hogan, you don't want to be raising my patient's blood pressure."

"Yes, ma'am . . . er, I mean no, ma'am," Susan said, shifting herself from the bed to the visitor's chair.

After the nurse fussed over Jake, took his temperature and blood pressure and heart rate, Susan said, "I better be going. I'll go by Aunt Jenny's and see how things are and then go right home."

"Be sure you do. I'll worry about you."

"Jake Phillips, I am a perfectly capable adult woman, and I can take care of myself!"

"And how many times have I rescued you? Take care, Susan. I can't rescue you tonight, so don't even think about joining the sheriff's little search group."

"As if I would," she said haughtily and left, with a casual wave over her shoulder. No goodnight kiss.

But he had unknowingly planted the idea in her mind, the last thing he wanted to do.

Chapter Twelve

Susan Hogan was nobody's fool, nor was she a Lone Ranger type. She managed a calm bowl of soup with Aunt Jenny and the judge. Jenny reported that a woman from the church who did interior design was going to come by, look at the house, and take her fabric shopping in Fort Worth.

Before Susan could even speak, the judge was quick to say, "Whoa, Jenny! You ask her how much she charges for this service."

"Oh, she won't charge," Jenny said airily. "She's doing this out of the goodness of her heart."

This time Susan joined the judge in a chorus. "I doubt that. You ask. No, wait. I'll make the call. Tell me her name and number."

After scratching around in her purse, Aunt Jenny supplied the information, and Susan called. When she hung up and turned to Aunt Jenny, she tried to keep the triumph out of her voice. "Five hundred dollars."

"Five hundred dollars? I can't pay that." Jenny was aghast.

"Now, Jenny. The insurance will repay you."

"I thought she was doing it as a kindness to me. No, I won't pay. But, where will I go for fabric?"

Susan said she'd take her to Cutting Corners in Fort Worth.

Meantime, Susan itched to get home and call Ellen Peck, her sometimes partner-in-crime. Driving home, she punched in Ellen's number—*don't look at me driving and talking, Jake. What you don't know won't hurt you.*

Ellen answered with a cheerful question about Jake, and Susan assured her he was on the mend and should be discharged the next day.

"I'm headed home now," Susan said. "Why don't you come have a glass of wine with me? I'll catch you up on all the details."

Ellen knew Susan well enough to be cautious. "The last time you caught me up on details, I ended up in the hospital with a punctured lung and broken rib."

"Nothing like that," Susan said. "I just need a sounding board, and you're so good at helping me sort things out in my mind."

Eventually, reluctantly, Ellen agreed to be at Susan's house in thirty minutes.

Susan pulled some cream cheese and chutney from the fridge, checking the chutney for date, and put out a snack tray with two wine glasses and a cool bottle of sauvignon blanc. By the time Ellen arrived, Susan was wearing a sort of one-piece loungewear garment Jake had bought her though she protested she'd never wear it.

"I smell a rat," Ellen said, taking in the carefully set scene.

"Oh, come on. Let's go out on the deck."

So they did. Ellen, of course, knew the story about Aunt Jenny and the dog and Jesse and Amanda. But she didn't know about the arrest of the two open-carry women nor the fact that one apparently shot Jake deliberately and was probably also the one who called him about Jesse's body. She listened intently as Susan reeled off these details, and then asked, "Why would she shoot Jake? Surely it doesn't have anything to do with Jesse's death."

Susan appeared to think this over. "I don't know. Maybe she cared about Jesse."

"Isn't there a bit of an age gap there?" Ellen looked skeptical.

"Can't tell with these women. They don't fix themselves up much."

"Doesn't sound like Jesse's idea of a woman—he liked them lean and blonde and classy."

"Well, it gets stranger. I'm convinced that Jesse's death is related to those open-carry people, whether it was that woman or not. I think he fell in with that crowd, maybe liked the idea of carrying a rifle. But his older brother, Gus, is like their father—strongly opposed to firearms of any kind. Well, here's what's funny.

"Everyone's wondering that these open-carry people rent rooms all over town. There's some talk that they must have a meeting place or something out in the country. Tonight, I saw their leader—I call him Pigface—in the grocery and followed him way out past my house until he turned on a county road."

"Susan! You know how dangerous that is."

"I was very careful, kept my distance, kept going when he turned, and then doubled back." Susan talked rapidly, justifying her actions. "Anyway, I found a dirt road marked 'Private Property—Trespassers will be Shot.' Not much else on the road, so I figure that's where he went. 'Course I couldn't see anything because that road led into some dense brush. I went on by, doubled back, and just as I came to the road, Gus Conroy roared out of there on a motorcycle.

Now why would Gus be visiting the people who killed his brother?"

"Susan, you don't know that. You just manufactured it in your mind."

"I definitely know there's a connection between the Conroy brothers and Pigface. You know Aunt Jenny's dog? The one Gus Conroy brought her? Pigface came to my house, claiming he'd lost his dog and was desperate to find her. Why target the two of us? I watched—he didn't go to any other houses on my block. And then, Aunt Jenny's house was tossed."

"Tossed?"

"Ransacked by someone looking for something. They tore up pillows, furniture, dumped garbage, knocked over lamps. It was an awful mess."

Ellen was on her feet in indignation. "Poor Aunt Jenny. Can I help her? Did they take the dog?"

Susan poured a little more wine for each of them. "That's the funny thing. Lucy was hiding in the backyard. Acted like she'd been beaten or terrorized. Won't get inches away from Aunt Jenny now."

Ellen sank back down in her chair. "Susan"—she fixed her with a direct gaze— "I wasn't smart enough to say this to you when we got in that mess after Missy Jackson was killed, but I am now. You're over your head in this. Leave it alone. The sheriff and Dirk Jordan are equipped to handle it, and Jake will be able to add his insight, even if he can't go out tracking gun carriers in the middle of the night. That's what you want to do, isn't it? Go prowling through those woods at night and find the hideout or whatever you'd call it."

Susan forgot to be coy, tactful, any of those things. "Don't you see? Jake may get out of the hospital tomorrow, and he'll come here. I have to go tonight. I won't be able to get away from him after that. I need you to go with me."

"No way." Ellen crossed her arms over her chest and gave Susan her most determined look. "Fool me once, shame on you; fool me twice, shame on me."

"But, Ellen, I have to go. I owe it to Gus Conroy and Amanda and a lot of other people to find out what's going on."

Ellen shook her head. "You owe it to Jake and Aunt Jenny and the judge and even me to keep yourself safe. That's first."

The two women were at an impasse, and each regarded the other with stony silence. Finally, after a long time, they reached a compromise. Ellen would drive and would stay in the car, with her cell phone on. Susan would creep silently— Ellen thought crash was a better word but didn't say it— through the woods, carrying the torch-like flashlight but keeping it off. It was as much a weapon as a light. They would go at ten that night.

Susan nearly fell on her knees with gratitude, but Ellen said to wait until they were both safe in the wee hours before she got too grateful.

* * * *

Ellen drove into Susan's driveway just before ten that night. Like Susan, she was dressed in black, but unlike Susan she had a grim expression on her face, her mouth drawn tight like a slash across her face. Susan, by contrast, was wide-eyed with anticipation . . . and a lot of apprehension. She carried the flashlight and had stuck her cell phone in the pocket of a jacket that was almost too warm for the night.

Ellen did not say a word as Susan got in the car, just headed out the highway. Finally, "Tell me where to turn."

"I will. It's still a bit farther. And when you turn, douse the lights."

Ellen rolled her eyes. "Swell, drive on one of our poorly maintained county roads on a dark night with no headlights."

She was right about one thing. It was a dark night. A thick bank of clouds covered stars and moon. Susan thought that a blessing.

Finally, "That left up ahead. Almost unmarked."

Ellen turned and cut the lights, driving so slowly Susan thought she'd have a heart attack.

Susan spotted the road with its No Trespassing sign and signaled Ellen to keep going until she could turn around.

"In the dark, with no lights? We'll end up in the bar ditch." She clutched the wheel tightly.

"I can show you a wide place, and, besides, your car is small like mine, can turn on a dime."

"Cold comfort," Ellen muttered.

Susan directed her where to turn, but Ellen did it in such small circles that Susan was sure it would be midnight before they got headed the other way. Finally, they crept back toward the highway, and about a hundred yards from the dirt road, Susan whispered dramatically, "Stop. Wait right here."

She crawled out of the car, barely closing the door, and carefully felt her way across the bar ditch. In minutes, she was back. "Damn! Barbed wire. I don't want to fight with that in the dark. Go ahead and stop well this side of the dirt road."

"Aye, aye, captain." There wasn't a trace of humor in Ellen's sarcasm. "I swear, Susan, if either of us end in the hospital again . . ."

"We won't, and I won't be gone long. Just wait—but don't read email on your phone or anything—lights would be a giveaway."

Ellen said nothing as Susan got out of the car, crossed the ditch again, and headed toward the dirt road that had no gate—just that threatening trespassing sign. Once onto the road and past the barbed wire, she hoped to melt quietly into the brush. It was not to be. Dry branches crackled under her feet, a stray branch smacked her in the face, causing her to yelp in pain, and she decided she was about as quiet as a herd of elephants. But a good way ahead, she saw lights from a window that appeared to have paper pasted over it, so that the light was a mere glow. And she smelled something—a chemical smell, or maybe cat urine, with which she was all too familiar from Aunt Jenny's cats over the years.

Susan paused to consider, her hand on a fallen tree trunk. Maybe she had seen enough to report to Jake and Dirk and the sheriff. She wasn't sure she'd see any more up close if the windows were covered, and the smell was making her dizzy. Besides, the woods were beginning to spook her—was that a branch falling, a footstep, or just her imagination? Her breathing was shallow and rapid, and she feared for a moment she might pass out. Then how would Ellen find her?

Taking a deep breath, she moved a few steps forward and was about to come to the end of the trees, where a large patch of open land stood between her and the cabin. Did she have the nerve to cross it? What if she heard a rifle shot?

As she was about to take another step forward a hand in a dirty glove clamped over her mouth, and an arm encircled her shoulders.

"Shhh, Doctor Hogan. Don't say a word. They know there's someone out here, and they sent me to investigate. I never expected to find you." It was Gus Conroy, who removed his dirty glove from her face immediately.

Without another word, he took her hand and led her toward the road. Susan realized she had become hopelessly disoriented and might well not have found her way back.

"You don't want to walk down that dirt path," Gus whispered. "Motion sensitive cameras." After a minute, still stage-whispering, "How did you get here?"

"A friend is waiting in her car."

"I'll see you to that car, and then we'll talk later. Just get in it, keep the lights off, and get out of here quick as you can."

Just before Gus eased the car door shut after her, she heard an angry voice calling, "Gus, where the hell are you? What'd you find?"

Ellen had providentially kept the motor idling, so there was no sound of a car starting. She put it in gear and they glided out toward the highway, where she insisted on turning on the headlights. "I'm not driving a dark car on the highway with no lights."

Susan was grateful for the brush that she hoped screened the cabin from the highway. But she rolled her window down ever so slightly to hear any more shouts from the woods. Instead, she heard the clear crack of one rifle shot. And then she screamed and screamed.

Ellen drove furiously. "Stop, Susan! You'll have them on our tail. Shut up!" She went so far as to take one hand off the wheel and lightly slap Susan in the face.

Susan stopped screaming and began to cry softly. "Did they shoot Gus? What if that's what happened? And it's all my fault." She dropped her face in her hands and began to sob.

Ellen refrained from saying, "I told you this was a bad idea." But it was hard for her. Instead, she asked, "Where to now? It's too late for you to see Jake."

"Home," Susan muttered. "I want to go home. Ellen, please say you'll come in with me. I . . . I need to talk to someone."

Ellen wanted to say, "It's not me," but instead she replied, "For a few minutes."

Once they were inside, Susan got down Jake's bourbon bottle and poured herself two fingers neat. Ellen declined in favor of a glass of wine.

Susan, prickly, independent Susan, was a complete mess. "What should I do? Call Jake? Call the sheriff about the rifle shot? Either way I'll have to confess what I was doing tonight. I can't do it." She began to pace back and forth in the tiny kitchen area.

"Susan, try not doing anything. It's too late to call Jake, nearly midnight, and you have no real grounds to call the sheriff. One rifle shot does not a murder make."

"But what if Pigface shot Gus? Mrs. Conroy couldn't stand the loss of her only surviving son."

"Susan! You're bringing your bridges up too close and jumping them. You have no idea what happened."

"But I have a good imagination."

"That's the trouble with English majors. We all have good imaginations."

A knock on the front door froze both women.

"What shall we do?" Susan asked.

"I guess I'd go see who it is, cell phone in hand," Ellen replied practically.

Her heart in her mouth, Susan inched toward the front door. Standing sideways, she peeked out the glass. Gus Conroy stood there.

With a whoop, Susan threw open the door, threw her arms around the young man, and said, "Oh, Gus, you're not dead!"

Chapter Thirteen

Gus, more emboldened than Susan had ever seen him, said, "No, I'm not dead, but I came closer than I want to think about."

In a calm, collected manner, Susan said, "It's all my fault." She expected denial and was startled when Gus said,

"Yes, ma'am. It surely is. What were you doing out there tonight?"

"I . . . well . . . I followed Pinkston out there earlier, and I wanted to see where he was going. Then I saw you roar out of that private road on a motorcycle."

Gus put a hand on his head, as if to ward off a headache. "If only I'd seen you, I could have stopped this whole mess." He sat at the kitchen counter, remembered his manners, and reached a hand toward Ellen. "I'm Gus Conroy."

"I figured that out. I'm Ellen Peck."

"Nice to meet you. Why did you drive Doctor Hogan out there tonight?"

Ellen threw her hands heavenward, as if to say there was no logical explanation.

Gus said, "Pinkston heard a noise and sent me out to look for whatever caused it. Then he thought I was gone too long, and I probably was because I was helping you. He came out of that pigsty cabin just as I came back, and I told him it was a good-sized buck. I figured that would interest him, a buck that close, and he'd want to go hunting in the morning. But he didn't believe me." Gus ran a nervous hand through his hair.

"Said if it was a buck, I was a doe, and if I ever double-crossed him, I'd end up the same as Jesse. He shot at me, deliberately missing—he's a good shot—but he darned near parted my hair for me. That's when you ladies turned onto the highway, turned your lights on, and Doctor Hogan screamed."

"I was afraid he shot you," Susan said.

"He damn near did, but he had an old single-shot rifle and had to go inside to reload. I was long gone when he came out. But he knows, Doctor Hogan, he knows you're stalking him."

"And why wouldn't I be? One of his women shot my partner, and he's tried to steal my aunt's dog." She got up and retrieved a beer from the refrigerator, which she silently handed to him.

"Thanks." A pause, and then, "I don't know what the deal is about that dog. I stole it from him. Yeah, Doctor Hogan, I lied to your Aunt Jenny, but Pinkston was so mean to Lucy—I like that name. He kept her tied up with that heavy collar on, and sometimes he kicked her for no reason. I saw to it that she was fed and had water, but one day when he was in town, I just took the dog. I couldn't see her treated like that anymore. She's just a puppy."

"I've got to go home, but I can't bear to miss any more of this," Ellen said out of nowhere.

"I wouldn't go now, ma'am. I 'spect they're outside watching this house . . . and maybe Aunt Jenny's."

Susan's alarm bells went off, and she immediately called Aunt Jenny's. "Judge, is everything all right? There's been a bit of trouble tonight—no, no, not here; I'm safe—but I just want to make sure no one is lurking around your house."

A pause while the judge talked softly into the phone.

"Okay," Susan said. "If anything alarms you, call Dirk Jordan. What?" Another pause. "I don't think Dirk Jordan will care one iota what you're doing there at nearly midnight."

She disconnected and turned to the other two. "Judge hasn't seen anything but said Lucy was really upset about a half an hour ago. And that bothered Aunt Jenny so much she went to bed. The judge said he wouldn't let Lucy out except on a leash in the back yard."

"Good," Gus said. "I hope he has a pistol."

"He does," Susan assured him.

"Can you ladies pretend to get ready for bed—turn out all the lights in this part of the house, maybe lights in the bedroom and bathroom. I want to look out and see what's happening."

"Won't they recognize your motorcycle?"

"Nope. It's in your garage, where you never park your car."

Susan shot him the first amused look of the evening. But her question was sobering. "Do you have a gun?"

"Nope. Don't believe in them. Don't worry. If I see anything suspicious, I'm going to suggest you call some authority."

Susan and Ellen went to the bedroom wing of the house, with Susan saying, "You might as well spend the night. I'll get you some jammies."

"Susan, I'd swim in your jammies. Get me a long T-shirt."

"With Gus in the house?" She returned with one of her never-worn nightgowns, which Ellen eyed skeptically.

Gus called softly from the front of the house. "Two cars, no lights. I recognize one as the old Plymouth Pinkston loves to drive around town. Don't know the other one. Doctor Hogan, go in your room and call Lieutenant Jordan on your cell, but tell him, if he'll listen, no sirens, no horns, none of that hero stuff. Maybe even no lights."

Susan found it strange to be taking orders from Gus, who had previously seemed sort of mild and retiring. But she did as she was told. And Dirk Jordan asked no questions, just said he'd be there.

Susan, Ellen, and Gus found themselves on the floor in the living room, just barely peeking over the windowsill to see what was going on. Dirk Jordan was as good as his word—a silent, no-lights approach until all of a sudden, his car was behind Pinkston's. The lights blazed and over the loudspeaker he said, "Do not drive that car away. Stay in the car. We have a rifle trained on you."

No movement from either Pinkston's car or the other one; another police vehicle had driven up behind the second car.

Jordan got out of his car and walked deliberately to Pinkston's driver's side, no weapon in sight. Susan's heart was in her throat, her mouth open, begging him not to take that risk. But Pinkston got out of his car with open hands, no rifle over his shoulder, and apparently surrendered his driver's license and insurance papers readily. Susan wished she were a fly on the wall so she could hear their conversation.

After a minute or two of talk, Jordan gestured toward the other car. Pinkston turned his head and apparently barked a command, because a younger man with a ponytail got out of the car, hands in the air, no rifle, and sauntered toward Jordan. Susan held her breath—Dirk was now out there with two of them and apparently, no backup except the second police car. She recognized the other man—the one she'd seen in the grocery store a week ago with Pinkston. Could it possibly be only a week?

Whispering to Gus, even though she knew the whisper was unnecessary, she asked, "Who is the other man?"

It startled her when Gus answered in a normal tone, even though his was a soft-spoken voice. "All I know is Pinkston calls him Squirrel. Don't know why. No idea what his proper name is. He's sort of Pinkston's second-in-command."

"Oh," Susan breathed softly, "good to know. I guess."

Ellen remained silent through all this, until she finally said, in tones Susan thought were definitely too loud, "Susan, you've got me in the middle of a mess again. I'm going home."

Gus was pleading. "I wouldn't do that right now, Doctor Peck. Wait until they're gone."

"They might stay there all night. No law against parking on a public street."

Gus agreed but said, "I think Jordan will run them off."

And he did. After some paperwork on Jordan's part, Pinkston and Squirrel roared off, gunning their motors as if in defiance. Dirk Jordan headed for Susan's house, and she met him at the front door.

"I was so frightened for you to confront those two without a weapon."

"They weren't gonna do anything," he said. "But they were spying on you. I ticketed them for loitering. Now tell me what went on tonight."

Susan tried to play innocent. "What do you mean? Ellen Peck and I were having a companionable glass of wine, and Gus just happened to drop by to say hello."

"At nearly midnight? I'm not buying that. Besides, I got other reports. Let's hear it, Susan."

His commanding use of her first name startled her, and the story of the evening came tumbling out. "I didn't call you because it's outside your jurisdiction, but Sheriff Wainwright didn't seem inclined to do anything about it."

Jordan pretended to be dumbfounded. "I wonder why." Then, "Conroy, you want to tell her?"

"I . . . I . . . I'm helping the sheriff and Lieutenant Jordan. You might call me undercover, though that sounds . . . well, like something more important than it is." He hung his head, as though what he had said was something shameful, and Susan had a hard time imagining him as a tough undercover agent.

"They know you're Jesse's brother. Doesn't that make them suspicious?"

"Oh, no, ma'am. I was hanging out with them before Jesse was killed because I knew he was there, and I wanted to keep him out of trouble. Jesse liked excitement, and I think he saw Pinkston and his bunch as living on the edge, a dramatic change from campus life. As for protecting him, I guess I didn't do a very good job."

"Nonsense," Dirk said. "You did the best you could. Jesse, forgive me, made his own fate. It was his nature. But what you tell us now is valuable. We've got to figure a way to get by tonight and still make it work." The look he threw at Susan was accusatory.

"I've ruined your plan, haven't I?" she asked.

"Well, I don't know you've ruined it, but you've put a big crimp in it. And Pinkston sees you as a big threat now."

"He should. One of his ladies shot Jake in the stomach." Anger boiled up in her again.

Her phone rang, and she saw it was Jake.

"How are you calling me at midnight? Don't they have a curfew at that place?"

"Thanks, Susan. I'm glad to talk to you tonight too. Where the hell have you been?"

Susan hesitated too long.

"Susan, I know you've been up to something. Tell me."

"Here," she said, "talk to Dirk Jordan. I can't retell it again."

Dirk gave Jake an abbreviated version of the night's events. There were some mumbled, "Yeah," and "I suspect" and other phrases that Susan heard but could not tie to any-thing specific. Finally, Dirk handed the phone back to Susan.

Instead of waiting for Jake to scold her, she went on the attack. "You knew about this all along, and you didn't tell me."

His voice was weary, not physical tiredness from his condition, but mental fatigue from having gone over simi-lar grounds with her so often. "Yes, I knew. I'm a law en-forcement officer, Susan, even though you may think of me as the campus cop."

She bit her tongue to hold back the protest that sprang to mind.

"I work with my fellow law enforcement officers, and since I have always been part of Jesse's death, they called me in on this. I saw no reason to tell you. In fact, I saw trouble if I told you. Apparently, that was the wrong call on my part."

"I've screwed it up, haven't I?" She sounded a bit repentant.

"Royally," he said.

Out of the corner of her eye she saw Dirk Jordan semi-salute her as he went out the door, whispering something to Ellen. Gus followed him and Ellen silently turned toward the bedrooms.

"Susan, I'm being dismissed tomorrow, but I need to go somewhere that I can get care. Shall I go to Aunt Jenny's?"

"No. I'll make up the guest room for you." Her tone was frosty.

"Awww, Susan . . ."

"You're recovering from a gunshot, Jake. I wouldn't want to attack you in the night and ruin your healing. I'll call in the morning and see what time you'll be dismissed."

"It's always afternoon," he said. "Susan? I love you."

"Give me time, Jake. It's been a bad evening. I'll see you tomorrow. Aunt Jenny's making meatloaf."

"Yeah, I know. I talked to John tonight . . . a few times."

She disconnected, fighting back tears.

"Susan, don't shoot yourself in the foot," Ellen said.

Susan dropped on the couch. "I know. I just feel such a fool right now."

"Forget it. We had an adventure, and it went a little wrong. We didn't know. I'm spending the night, after all. Lieutenant Jordan's orders."

Susan nodded, then said, "I'll have to make the bed up for Jake tomorrow."

Ellen said, "I'll help" and Susan suddenly remembered what was important. "Thanks, Ellen. Thanks for staying, for going with me tonight on a fool's errand, and for always being there for me."

Ellen came and wrapped her arms around a resistant Susan. "I'm glad to do it. Just tell Aunt Jenny I particularly love King Ranch chicken."

Chapter Fourteen

The next morning was Saturday. Susan woke early, frustrated that she couldn't go back to sleep on a morning when she usually slept late. Ellen had come in at first light to say she was going home and urge Susan not to do anything foolish.

Lying in bed, Susan contemplated the day. She'd have to go get Jake, but what could she say to him, how should she act? He was angry at her, no doubt about that. But she was angry at him, mostly because she needed someone to blame for the fact that she'd done something she really shouldn't have. It wasn't Jake's fault, but for a moment she tried to make it seem that way.

And Gus? Was his life in danger now? She thought about Aunt Jenny's description of Mrs. Conroy and knew that poor woman couldn't stand to lose another son. And because Susan had blundered unknowingly into a situation more dangerous than she could have believed. It was, she convinced herself, all Jake's fault.

On impulse, her first call was to Dirk Jordan. When he answered in his usual clipped voice, she demanded, "How much danger is Gus Conroy in?"

"Good morning, Susan," he said smoothly. "I'd say the boy is in a lot of danger—from a sniper, if nothing else. I want him to leave town, but he refuses because of his parents and his job. He thinks he has great possibilities for advancement in the grocery business."

"Hah! What, store manager?"

Dirk's voice was sharp. "He's always seen himself in Jesse's shadow. I bet if Gus got an education, he could do almost anything. He's a bright boy, with good solid instincts. He's been a big help to us so far."

"And I ruined it and put his life in danger."

No hesitation on the other end. "Essentially, yes. But you also put your own life in danger. I don't think these people are fooling around."

Susan sat bolt upright in bed, glad that the phone was not on Facetime. "Why are they so serious about open carry that they'd kill someone? That makes no sense. They say they want people to feel comfortable around guns."

"There's more to it than that, Susan. Much more."

"What?"

"I won't be the one to tell you. Talk to Jake. When is he out of the hospital?"

"Today, if he hasn't worked himself into a snit and raised his blood pressure."

"Good. I'll feel better when he's there with you."

"Hah! Some protection he'll be. I'll have to protect him." She knew deep in her heart it would never work out that way.

"Susan, just go get him out of the hospital and try not to raise his blood pressure. I'll take care of protecting you and Gus."

She disconnected the call, took a long shower, lingered over coffee and the slim Oak Grove newspaper, even watched a cooking show on TV. But nothing made time pass. And Jake didn't call. Finally, she put on jeans, a plaid button-down shirt, athletic shoes, and started for the hospital.

Within minutes out of her driveway, she realized some-one was following her. Not Pinkston, or at least not his car, but she didn't know who until at a stoplight the person pulled right up behind her. *Not skilled at subtle following, are you?* With a start, she realized that the driver of the car behind her had long hair—one of Pinkston's two women followers. It couldn't be the one who shot Jake—she was safely in jail—so it must be the other one. She knew well enough that one of them wasn't hesitant to shoot, and she suspected the other one wasn't either. Hairs prickled on the back of her neck, and a great shiver went through her body.

For reasons she could never explain later, she changed her course and drove to Aunt Jenny's. The judge's car was in the driveway, so she parked behind it and had to force herself to walk not run to the front door, feeling all the while there was a bull's-eye on her back.

The other car kept going, slowly. Susan watched spell-bound as it went down the block, turned around in the intersection, and headed back. Then she bolted inside the unlocked front door and quickly turned to lock it.

"Susan, whatever is the matter with you?" Aunt Jenny jumped up from the couch where she'd apparently been needlepointing.

"You all right, girl?" the judge asked, peering over the top of his reading glasses and the newspaper in his lap.

"Don't you ever lock this door?" Susan demanded. "With the trouble you've had, I'd think you'd keep it double-bolted all the time." She turned to pull the window curtain aside just enough to allow her a view of the car, now sitting outside the house. Her knees felt like jelly.

The judge strolled over to the window, pulled the curtain full back, and asked, "Who's in the car?"

Susan found her voice was shaky. "One of the two women with the open-carry people. It must be the one who didn't shoot Jake."

"Jenny, make Susan a cup of tea—put plenty of honey in it. She needs the sugar. I'm calling Dirk Jordan."

Susan listened as he said, "Dirk, you might want to get over here. Seems like one of the women with the open-carry people followed Susan over here and is now sitting outside, staring at the house." A pause. "Okay, thanks. No, the dog is in the house. She always is," he added wryly.

Turning to Susan, he said, "I saw once where someone trained a dog to use the toilet. I'm thinking that would be a good idea for Lucy, since Jenny won't let her out of her sight."

Susan looked at him in amazement. How could he joke at a time like this?

* * * *

By the time Dirk Jordan arrived, the woman in the car had fired a random rifle shot at a front window. The bullet ricocheted off the wall and did little damage except to Aunt Jenny's favorite teapot.

After she stopped sobbing, Aunt Jenny declared, "I'm moving back to Wichita Falls. This is too dangerous a town."

The judge was fully occupied trying to calm Aunt Jenny and Susan sat stunned, staring into space when Dirk Jordan rang the doorbell—insistently. Susan detected an impatient urgency to his pressing on the button and hurried to open the door.

"What's that?" he asked, pointing to the shattered window.

Susan got enough of her wits about her to say, "A broken window. Shot out. Bullet's in here someplace—shattered Aunt Jenny's favorite teapot."

He favored her with a sardonic look and took out his phone, calling for backup. "The woman who followed you did this?"

"That would be my logical assumption," Susan said. In her mind, there was no other explanation, and she thought his question unnecessary.

"Why did you come here instead of going to the hospital?"

Susan shrugged. That was a hard one to answer, and it meant admitting some of her childhood insecurity. "Aunt Jenny is always where I go when I need security."

Jordan was now downright scornful. "It didn't occur to you that you'd put her in danger and that a public place like the hospital would be safer?"

She looked at the floor. "No, it didn't. I was scared, and I wasn't thinking clearly." Then she looked at him almost defiantly. "Why did she shoot? No one was at the window. She had no target. She just fired."

"Exactly. She fired because she could. It was threatening, and it was a statement of her power. Do you believe me these people mean business now?"

"I believe you, but I don't understand why."

"I'm sending someone to get Jake out of the hospital and bring him here. Then we'll all sit and talk about it. Meantime, go make some tea, fix sandwiches, do whatever women are supposed to do in times of crisis."

Susan wanted to retort that the word "crisis" was a bit harsh, but she looked at Aunt Jenny, who was still safe in the judge's arms, and bit back her comment. "Aunt Jenny, do you have a couple of cans of tuna and a lot of bread?"

Jenny nodded yes, and Susan took herself off to the kitchen. Tuna salad was one thing she could make successfully, if she could keep Jake from putting pickle in it. By the time she had made some sandwiches, the house was swarming with police officers, combing the place for that bullet. She put the sandwiches on a tray, made a pitcher of lemonade, and put it all on Aunt Jenny's dining table with napkins.

When she heard a loud "Here it is!" she turned and thought, *wouldn't you know Jordan would be the one to find it!*

He bagged the bullet, handed it to an assistant, and asked, "Are these for general consumption?" nodding toward the sandwiches.

"Of course," Susan replied. "When will Jake be here?"

"About five minutes. They just wheeled him out of the hospital."

Good, I can take him home and everything will be fine. Susan had a suspicion that wasn't the way things were going to work, and she was right. Somehow, she had expected Jake to stride into the house, hale and hearty as ever. Instead, an officer held his arm and helped him, and Jake walked slowly. He looked pale and thin, things she'd never noticed in the hospital.

Jordan saw to it that Jake was settled on the couch, and Susan reluctantly let go of her idea of their moment of happy reconciliation. She slipped quietly over to the couch, just as Aunt Jenny exclaimed, "Jake Phillips, you look awful!"

"Thanks, Aunt Jenny." His voice was wry. "I'm not feeling my best right now, matter of fact. And I'm curious . . . more than that . . . about what the hell is going on here."

"I'm moving back to Wichita Falls," Aunt Jenny was swift to reply, but the judge was equally quick. "No, you're not."

Like a schoolteacher, Dirk Jordan raised his hand for silence and began to relate what had happened that morning.

Susan felt she had been robbed of the chance to tell her own story. She sat at one end of the couch, next to Aunt Jenny, who kept squeezing her hand, and John, who sat ramrod straight at attention.

John interrupted in his commanding voice. "Lieutenant, I think we all know about Susan's adventure of last night and the results at her house. What about the sheriff's expedition to sneak up on those people?"

Jordan glared at him. "Cancelled. There was no sense carrying it out when they'd been forewarned. I've put out an arrest order for the woman who shot the window. At least we can get her for vandalism." He turned his glare briefly on Susan, who wished fervently for a hole in Aunt Jenny's couch to reach up and swallow her. The look Jake threw her was not encouraging.

With an ironic nod at the judge, Dirk went on, "If I may, the first thing we must look into is the safety of Jake and Susan. Jake, where will you be?"

"Damned if I know." He looked at both Aunt Jenny and Susan. "These ladies are settling my future between them. Frankly, I feel everybody involved would be safer if I stay at Susan's, as long as Aunt Jenny promises to cook my meals." Now he looked at Susan with just a hint of laughter in his eyes.

Jenny protested. "I could feed him better if he were here, and he'd be perfectly safe. John has a gun."

Dirk Jordan rolled his eyes.

After some discussion, during which Susan kept mostly quiet, Jake announced that he would stay at Susan's, *in the guest room,* and would Aunt Jenny please make him soup and that meatloaf he requested. She agreed.

They hashed out safety plans. Jake would be responsible for his own safety— "it's not like this is for more than a day or two," he protested—and he would arrange for on-campus protection for Susan. She was instructed to be watchful any time she was not one of the two places. "Give your aunt any grocery list for a few days until we get this wrapped up."

Susan fumed silently. Of course, she knew enough to watch for tails in the car, etc. Did he think she was a bimbo? Silently, she agreed with herself—yes, he probably did! After all, she hadn't behaved brilliantly today.

Jordan went on. Gus would stay at Susan's on the couch—he had no place to go and refused to leave town. He and Jake could have a sort of mutual protection society.

Susan was now angry enough to speak up. "I agree with being cautious, but I refuse to be a sitting duck. What's the plan to arrest these dangerous people and find out who murdered Jesse?"

Jordan cut her off with an abrupt, "Don't worry about that. We'll take care of it."

Later, she thought Jake would have found himself sleeping in the garage, let alone the guest room, if he hadn't spoken up. "Wait a minute, Jordan. This is Wainwright's case, not yours, not mine. We can sit here and plan protection but we have no authority to direct the investigation."

Dirk Jordan stammered, "Uh . . . of course. We'll work closely with the sheriff and do whatever he asks us to."

Which may well be to butt out of his case, Susan thought.

Chapter Fifteen

It was early evening by the time Susan and Jake got to her house. Gus was with them. They'd had Aunt Jenny's meatloaf for an early supper meal and had brought leftovers home for sandwiches, with Aunt Jenny's promise of meatball soup tomorrow ringing in their ears.

Now there was an air of discomfort in the house. Jake declared he was tired, so Gus helped him into the guest bedroom, and Susan settled him in the bed.

"I won't sleep long," he promised. He slept five hours.

Gus left for his grocery store, over Susan's protests that was the last place he should go. Pinkston would surely look for him there.

"Miss Hogan, I can't and I won't live in fear. I will be cautious. But I need to tell my boss what's going on—in person. And then I'll go check on my mom. I know she's frantic with worry."

So there Susan was, alone with a sleeping invalid. Back in the living room, Susan wandered from pillar to post, uncertain what to do with herself. No need to cook. She surely wasn't going to start cleaning house or anything extreme like that. She could finish grading those Frost essays, but she had a hard time concentrating. Finally, she settled in the recliner with Sheila Connolly's newest orchard mystery, *Seeds of Deception.*

Her mind wandered. She had missed Jake so much, missed his physical presence, and she couldn't wait to have her hands on him, to touch him—not in an arousing way but with love and compassion and longing. He had not touched her since he got out of the hospital—was that deliberate or was he so caught up in what was going on? When she heard the first stirrings from the guest room, it was nearing midnight, and she went in and sat on the edge of the bed, reaching for the hand closest to her.

"I missed you . . . a lot," she said tentatively.

To her joy, he reached up, tousled her spiky hair, and said "I missed you too. And this bed is lonely. I'm sleeping in your bed tonight. Will you wear one of my T-shirts?"

"Yes, but I promise not to touch you."

"Well, damn!"

They were back on their old footing. Gus came in about midnight, and they ate meatloaf sandwiches. Susan reheated the green bean casserole but Jake complained it was never as good reheated.

"The French-fried onions get soggy."

"Tastes pretty good to me," Gus said, taking a large helping.

Susan stacked the dishes and the three of them sat around talking about Pinkston and his minions, until Jake said, "Gus, I'm going to bid you goodnight. Getting out of the hospital is more exhausting than I thought. I gotta go to bed."

"Oh, yes, sir." Gus jumped to his feet. "I'm sorry I kept you so late."

Susan stole a quick look at her watch—it was after one o'clock. "Gus, I thought you were sleeping here, so Jake could protect us both."

Gus blushed to the roots of his hair. "Oh, no, ma'am. You and Mr. Jake, you need your privacy. I'll be safe. Don't you worry none."

"Where will you go?"

He was evasive. "I'm not sure, but I won't go home. I promise you that."

Jake put a hand on her arm, and she knew he was signaling her to drop the subject. She showed Gus out the front door, begged him again to be safe, and then helped Jake to her bed. "You're sure?"

"I'm sure," he said. "Go put that T-shirt on."

She did. It was a huge, faded Dallas Cowboys T-shirt. Susan hated football.

They slept holding hands, Susan always wakeful to see that she didn't hurt Jake. Pinkston and his minions were far from her mind, and she had no idea that a strange truck was in her driveway. Someone was watching them.

* * * *

Next morning, they slept late. Susan woke to find Jake staring at her. After a long minute, he spoke. "Susan, don't put yourself in Pinkston's path. I couldn't stand it if anything happened to you."

She sat up and leaned down to kiss him.

"Where's my coffee, woman?" he demanded.

When she went into the kitchen to start the coffee, Susan noticed the truck in her driveway. "Jake? Gus spent the night in our driveway. He was protecting us and not the other way around."

"Fool kid. He was a sitting duck for Pinkston. Would you go bring him in the house?"

"In your T-shirt?"

"You might put some jeans on," he conceded.

She followed the coffee with soft scrambled eggs that Gus ate heartily and Jake was adamant about not eating and she was equally firm he would eat.

"You don't know how bad the eggs were in the hospital," he whined. He picked and finally ate most of them—with picante sauce, which Susan declared was not good for his stomach at all.

"So you were worried about me?" Jake leaned on the counter and looked at her. "Worried enough to say we could talk about a dog?"

Gus looked uneasy. "I got to go to the store. I'll leave you guys to your discussion of dogs."

"Son," Jake adopted a fatherly attitude that probably irritated Gus. Jake wasn't *that* much older. Gus interrupted him before he could finish whatever he was going to say.

"I'll be fine, and I have to go if I want to keep my job. Besides, Pinkston and those folks stay up late and sleep late. They won't be around."

"You be extra watchful. Call me if you need to."

Susan wondered what good Jake would do. He was still weak from his hospital stay, though he showed signs of regaining his strength quickly. She turned to Gus. "Take care."

"Where was I?" Jake asked aloud. "Oh yes, you missed me?"

"You know I did. What's your point?"

"I heard," he said, "that you were worried enough that you said if I survived you were willing to talk about a dog."

She bit her tongue, because she remembered asking the doctor to give Jake that message. "Well," she prevaricated, "we might begin to talk about it."

"Good." He came back around the counter and sat down. "I've been thinking a lot about this. I think we need a German Shepherd."

She drew in a sharp breath. And was silent for a minute and then said slowly, "Sometimes they're, ah, unpredictable."

"Not if they're trained right," he said confidently.

"And who will train this dog? You want a pup, I assume."

"Yeah, a puppy so it can grow up with us. And I'll train it."

"You don't have time."

Jake gave her a long look. "Susan, what kind of dog do you want?"

"Something loveable. You know, a lab like Lucy. Maybe a collie."

"A collie," he said quickly. "They've had the brains all bred out of them in search of the perfect narrow face." A pause. "If I can have a say in picking the puppy I might consider a lab like Lucy. But I don't think Gus will find another dog . . ."

"How about a labradoodle?"

"Good golly, Susan. Do you know how much they cost?"

"They're supposed to be loyal and loving and protective but not aggressive."

"We pay half our income for the dog and then there'd be vet bills. We'd have to buy special food, toys for a pup, a good leather leash, a collar—collar! That's it!" He looked like lightning had struck. "Pinkston doesn't want the dog back—he wants the collar. I'm not sure why I didn't think of this before—any good campus lawman should be on the prowl for drugs all the time. Susan, you remember that old collar Lucy had? Aunt Jenny thought it was way too heavy and got a new one. What did she do with the old one?"

Susan shrugged. "I suppose she threw it away. Drugs? You're not serious?"

"I am, and I hope they didn't throw that collar away. It could be a strong clue and worth some money, enough to make people want it back," Jake said, reaching for his phone. In a moment, Susan heard him say, "Judge, I just thought of something. Remember that ugly heavy collar Lucy had when Gus brought her to Aunt Jenny. Where is it? You didn't throw it away, did you?" Apparently, the answer on the other end was not satisfactory, because Jake muttered, "I hope not," and disconnected. Looking up, he said, "Judge thinks they threw it in the trash at the pet store in Fort Worth. Too late for us to find it."

"Jake, why is it that important?"

Before he could answer, Jake's phone rang. He listened intently and then said, "We'll be right over. We've got to find it." Hanging up, he said urgently, "Let's go."

"Where?"

"Aunt Jenny's house. She told the judge the collar was still in her purse when they got home that day, but she doesn't remember what she did with 'that nasty thing.'"

"And why do we have to find it?" Susan was being hustled toward Jake's truck.

"It might be our ticket to shutting Pinkston and his gang down." He didn't explain, and she didn't ask.

Jake headed for his truck, and Susan was right behind him, physically forcing him to the passenger seat. "Doctor said no driving until he okays it," she reminded.

"Aw, Susan, I can drive." He almost whined, but she had to boost him into the seat, and he quit arguing. During the short crosstown trip, he focused intently on Susan's driving—he never, ever let her drive his truck—and now alternated between, "Can't you go any faster?" and "Watch your speed, Susan." His only other words were, "I hope Gus keeps himself safe. I have a feeling he knows the secret of the collar." Susan concentrated on her driving.

* * * *

Almost two hours later, the judge, Jake, and Susan sat in Aunt Jenny's living room, exhausted. They had searched every corner of that house. When Jake insisted they check the crawl space, she had even climbed down just far enough to shine the flashlight and see there was nothing but dirt and rocks and . . . was that rat droppings? Jake conceded it was unlikely Aunt Jenny would have put it down there. The same was true of the attic, but Susan and the judge pulled down the staircase and climbed it, the judge insisting all the while that Jenny never climbed the contraption. They took clothes out of the closets, searched pockets and discarded purses; they rearranged Aunt Jenny's kitchen cupboards, while she complained, "I won't be able to find anything. Susan Hogan, you put things back neat as I had them." Lucy watched all this with great curiosity.

"Jenny, can't you remember what you wore that day?" The judge was pleading.

Aunt Jenny sat in an overstuffed chair, wringing her hands. Now she shook her head. "No. Don't you remember what I wore?"

The judge threw his hands in the air in a gesture of surrender.

"Susan, you check pots in the shed, all that?" Jake was visibly discouraged and exhausted.

"Yep," she answered. Jake had assigned her to check the tiny backyard and small shed where Aunt Jenny kept flower-pots and the like. She had gone over the ground inch by inch, pulling plants to one side and the other, prowling in the monkey grass, hoping she didn't disturb a snake. And she'd come up empty-handed.

Wearily she stood, saying, "I'll go take one more look." She left the others sitting, staring into space in discouragement.

A long ten minutes later, a great shout went up outside. It was Susan, yelling, "I found it! I have it in my hand." Before anyone else could move, she burst through the back door and ran to the living room, waving the collar.

It wasn't quite the nasty, heavy, lumpy thing Aunt Jenny had described, but it was dirty—once-white fabric had grayed from oils on Lucy's neck and her habit of rolling in the dirt. The collar was, in fact, a neatly sewn tube of fabric, with leather ends that had hooks to link and attached to a leash. It was indeed heavy for the neck of a young pup. Most of the people watching would have thrown it away without a thought, and they didn't blame Aunt Jenny at all. Lucy came and sniffed but backed away, almost like she was frightened.

"Must remind her of Pinkston," the judge remarked.

"Any chance she could have gotten it off herself?"

"No!" Aunt Jenny was indignant. "I took it off in the pet store and never put it back on her."

Jake was impatient. "Where'd you find it, Susan?"

"In a corner of the shed—a dark corner, I might add. It was actually in a pot but someone had set another pot on top of it, like they were hiding the collar."

Heads swiveled toward Aunt Jenny, who asked, "Why would I hide it? I hated it, but I had no idea anyone else was interested in it. Why are you interested in it, Jake?"

He held out his hand for the collar and then, with his knife, carefully slit open the seam. The others watched in fascinated silence. Finally, he laid the collar flat, revealing countless tiny plastic bags, the size you put herbs in at the market. These bags held a white powder.

"Is that what I think it is?" the judge asked.

Jake nodded. "Coke. I don't know street value, can't even guess at the purity—or lack of it, but you're looking at a lot of money. Lucy was Pinkston's mule, as it were."

"Mule?" Aunt Jenny look genuinely puzzled but the others knew what Jake meant.

Jake dialed his phone and in a minute said, "Walt? Jake Phillips here. I have something you'll want—and will be interested in seeing." Pause. "Yes, I think it's worth a trip over here right now. I'm at Jenny Hogan's, 14 Oak Drive." Another pause. "Good. See you shortly." Disconnecting, he grumbled, "Some people are sure unappreciative. You do their work, and they grumble because you want them to interrupt a baseball game on TV."

With a start, Susan realized it was still Sunday.

Chapter Sixteen

Sheriff Wainwright forgot his grumpy displeasure when he saw why he was called out. Aunt Jenny, with her insistence on order in her life, had found a dark red velvet throw somewhere, put it on the coffee table, and neatly arranged the packets of white powder on it. She never thought about preserving fingerprints, and Jake realized neither had he in his haste to get into the collar. Any evidence on the bags was definitely compromised now. Another stumbling block in a case full of them.

After his first exclamation of "Omigod," the sheriff began to laugh. "First time I ever saw it displayed like fine jewelry," he said.

"We got 'em, don't we?" Susan asked enthusiastically.

The sheriff sat down heavily. "Can you prove Pinkston put this stuff in that collar?"

"Who else?" she asked.

"How about your young friend, Gus? He could have lifted the coke, put it in the collar, and given the dog to Miss Hogan for safekeeping of the collar. He may even be the one who hid it in the flowerpot."

Susan was immediately indignant. "Gus would never do that! He gave Lucy to Aunt Jenny to protect her."

Jake suppressed an urge to tell Susan to stifle. "He's right, Susan. We have no proof."

"Jake, you said Gus told you Pinkston probably thought Jesse had double-crossed him, and he actually had threatened the boy. Maybe this was the real double-cross—stealing the dog. He was actually gunning for Gus before he protected Susan when she blundered into our plans."

"Could be," Jake agreed.

The sheriff looked hard at Jake. "Suppose it's your case. What would you do next?"

"Question Gus before I go storming that hideaway—the longer we can put off a violent confrontation and the more we can learn before that, the better." Jake's answer came promptly.

"Bingo! We'll make a law enforcement officer out of you yet." The sheriff was grinning.

Susan stiffened. She'd never heard anyone say anything remotely negative about Jake's law enforcement abilities, and now this country sheriff . . . She glanced at Jake.

"Yeah, old man," he drawled, "we'll bring you into the twenty-first century yet."

The two turned serious and said they were going to find Gus– only then did it dawn on all of them that they hadn't seen him all day. He'd promised to touch base in the early afternoon but by then they were searching for the collar.

Sheriff Wainwright scooped up the small bags, apparently unimpressed by Aunt Jenny's artful arrangement, and put them in an evidence bag, though by now any fingerprints were useless. "Should have used gloves and an evidence bag"—he shot Jake a disapproving glance— "but it's too late now."

"I think it was too late from the moment others handled that collar, like Gus, Aunt Jenny, and the judge. Finger-prints wouldn't stick to those baggies. I'll go with Walt," Jake said. "Where will I find you, Susan?"

"You will not go with the sheriff," Susan said firmly. "You're on bed rest, and you'll go home with me."

The sheriff agreed. "Can't have a young whippersnap-per hampering me," he said.

Jake glared at both of them, but he went with Susan, though he was sure having let her drive his truck made him more nervous than driving in his weakened state would. When they were safely in her driveway, he admitted, "I didn't realize how weak I am."

Without sympathy, she said, "I told you not to stand and go through all those clothes in the closet, Superman."

Susan desperately wanted to set up her own search for Gus, but Jake would never forgive and forget. She didn't care much about what the sheriff thought, but she cared a whole lot about not angering Jake anymore.

Once Jake was soundly sleeping, she decided to call Ellen and urge her to come for wine so the time would pass. Of course, she hoped it would be a quick search, and they'd come to her house with Gus in tow. She'd order pizza for all of them. Something about pizza for Sunday supper went against the grain of everything Aunt Jenny had taught her, but she squelched that thought.

Ellen was hesitant. "Are you sure you don't have one of your schemes going?"

"Promise. I don't want to make Jake any angrier with me. He's sleeping, and I just need you to help me pass the time. I'm worried about Gus and . . . well, I'm worried about everybody."

In a short time, the two were seated at Susan's counter. "Bring me up to date," Ellen said, and Susan did.

Ellen was overwhelmed. "Wow! Pinkston and his followers are even nastier than you thought."

"And to think we put Aunt Jenny in danger and caused her all the difficulty of the break-in and then the shooting."

"Well, at least she doesn't have the coke now, so they won't bother her again," Ellen offered.

"They don't know she doesn't have it." Then Susan got a horrified look on her face. "We left them alone."

"Who?"

"Aunt Jenny and the judge."

"Susan, surely the judge will protect her."

"He will try, I know. He's got a gun. But Ellen, he's in his eighties. Grab your purse. We're going over there."

"Susan, you promised . . ."

"Oh, come on. What can happen? Jake can't possibly get mad because we went to Aunt Jenny's. We'll be back, and bring them, before he even wakes up."

"Angering Jake is the least of my worries." But Ellen had picked up her purse and headed for the door.

The two women were barely a block from Susan's house when she said, "Oh, swell. We've picked up a tail."

"Susan . . ." Fright marked Ellen's voice this time. She nervously turned around and then, just as quickly, whipped her head around to stare straight forward. "What will you do?"

"Ignore them. They just want to remind us they're still here."

"You'll lead them to Aunt Jenny," Ellen said, horrified.

"Ellen," Susan replied with all the patience she could muster, "they already know well enough where Aunt Jenny lives. Now they'll know she has reinforcements."

"Some reinforcements we are," Ellen muttered. "I was not prepared to reinforce anything today except my lesson plan."

The tail stayed with them, discreetly behind so Susan couldn't see who was driving but not so far back that she was unaware of the tail. When the two reached Aunt Jenny's house, the car sped off.

"See," Susan said.

Ellen was not reassured.

They had to make up some excuse to Aunt Jenny about why they were there, and then the four sat around the living room, Lucy going from one person to the other in search of affection. Conversation did not come easily and stalled completely when the phone rang.

The judge answered it in the kitchen—Aunt Jenny, of course, still had a landline and a wall phone. He held out the receiver and said, "Jenny. Gus' mother wants to talk to you."

Her face pinched into a worried frown, Jenny hurried to take the call. They heard her say, "Oh, my!" and "Yes, I'm sure you are." Then she straightened herself up and said, "Now Clara, I know Gus is all right. You just be patient, and he'll come home to you." A pause, and then, "And I want you to go to church with us. You'd meet some wonderful people our age." After a few more pleasantries, Jenny said goodbye and hung up.

"Aunt Jenny, you shouldn't hold out false hope to her. We have no idea if Gus is safe." Susan was a little angry with her aunt.

"Oh, he's all right. You be patient too, Susan. I'm going to start dinner. Something good and solid. We've had too much soup around here." She bustled off into the kitchen.

Ellen asked, "How can she be so cheerful and talk about church and food while the rest of us are wringing our hands with worry?"

"She knows something we don't," the judge said and picked up the newspaper to work the crossword puzzle, as though everything were perfectly fine.

* * * *

The sheriff and his deputy checked out the grocery store, drove around town, stopped by Subie's in the unlikely possibility that Gus had gotten hungry. They even went to the bar on the edge of town that students often frequented. There was no sign of Gus, and nobody they asked had seen him.

"He may be safely at his folks' house, though I don't think he'd go there and put them in danger. And I don't want to go there or even call. Don't want to cause that poor woman any more worry."

"How about Buster's shop?" the deputy suggested.

They found the mechanic's shop dark, with a sign that said "Closed." The two men tried all the doors to no avail and ended up peering in windows, knocking, and calling for Gus, assuring him who they were. After ten minutes, they gave up.

As they drove away, Wainwright's phone rang. He answered it and heard Buster Conroy on the other end. "You been prowling around my shop?"

"Yes, sir. Please don't tell Mrs. Conroy, but we can't find Gus, and I'm worried."

"She knows, but I told her she couldn't do a thing about it so she best quit fretting," Buster said and slammed down his old-fashioned phone.

Wainwright whistled. "He must have some sharp security system. There's one more place—Dudley's pasture, where we found that boy. I'll call Tish Hornsby and ask her to go back out there. She knows exactly where that old buffalo wallow is, and she has a four-wheel drive vehicle. Other than that, and it's a long shot, ol' Buster Conroy is right. The drug camp is the last place left, but I don't want to go out there yet. If that boy's there, he's either already dead or will be all right for a bit longer. We need backup and a plan."

He thought for a minute. "We'll go to my office and call Jordan and Jake." First, he called Doctor Hornsby, who suggested it wasn't in her usual duties but said she didn't want to deal with any more bodies of young boys. She'd go out there, look, and get back to him.

* * * *

When Wainwright roused him from a deep sleep, Jake woke to an empty house. Listening to the sheriff's plan, he asked him to have his meeting with Lieutenant Jordan at Susan's house, so he could be part of it. "I used whatever strength I've got looking for that damn collar," he explained.

Then he called Susan and found she was at Aunt Jenny's. She explained that she worried about her aunt and the judge. And then she asked a one-word question: "Gus?"

"Haven't found him yet, which is good news." Jake was glad she didn't see him. Susan was good at reading facial expressions and body language. "We've got a couple more ideas and places to check. Wainwright's gonna meet Jordan here and talk about a plan. I'll keep you posted."

* * * *

When Susan reported this to Aunt Jenny, the older woman said immediately, "Jake's worried, but this time he needn't be. I'm fixing supper for all of us. King Ranch Chicken." She beamed at Ellen. "I don't suppose the sheriff will stay for supper. He'll probably go home to eat with his wife."

Aunt Jenny had defrosted a chicken in the microwave. It always amused Susan that her old-fashioned aunt would do that. Jenny didn't like the microwave, muttered all the time it was operating, but she used it almost daily. She made a casserole with torn-up tortillas, diced chicken, creamed soups, Rotel tomatoes, and grated cheese. She was preparing to slide it in the oven, when there was a knock at the front door.

"Look before you open the door, John," she called out.

The judge gave her a look that clearly said he knew to do that. He looked through the peephole, let out a whoop, and opened the door for Gus.

Throwing his arms around the young man, he said, "Are we glad to see you!"

Gus looked puzzled.

* * * *

While law enforcement of Oak Grove was looking for him, Gus, unaware, was driving Amanda back to town from her Fort Worth doctor's appointment. Gone was the weepy, self-pitying girl he'd driven to Fort Worth. Amanda was clear-eyed, quiet. She sat almost without moving, her mouth set, her posture erect. And she was silent. Gus didn't push her. They were within ten miles of town when she spoke, her voice so low Gus had to strain to hear it.

"The baby is healthy so far, though it's too early to tell much. Sure can't tell the sex, but I hope it's a girl who looks like me. I don't need a daily reminder of Jesse for the rest of my life."

Jeff glanced at her. *Was this the same girl who'd cried on his shoulder almost every day?*

"Doctor says the most important thing right now is for me to stay healthy, physically and emotionally. I've got to eat right and make every effort to be happy, so I produce a happy baby, not a fretful one."

After a pause, she said, "I'm going home to tell my parents. And then I'm going to tell your parents."

Gus wanted to let go of the steering wheel long enough to clap, but he didn't. He opened his mouth to warn her about his father's probable reaction, but she cut him off.

"I know how your dad will be—worse than my dad. But I'm prepared for it. I'm going to raise this baby and finish school and be a responsible adult. I had a crush on Jesse. Someday I'll find real love."

Jesse thought that doctor must have done some fast talking. He liked Amanda better now than he had in their whole lives.

When he dropped Amanda at her parents' house, he offered to come in with her but she declined.

"My dad would probably try to make you marry me on the spot," she said with her first small smile of the day.

Gus rolled that idea around in his mind. Not a bad thought, but there were too many reasons he couldn't do that.

Chapter Seventeen

When Gus walked into Aunt Jenny's living room, he met a momentarily stunned and quiet audience. Then Susan and Aunt Jenny peppered him with questions, "Where have you been?" "Are you all right?" Followed by such statements as, "We were so worried about you," "Call your mother," and "Don't ever disappear again without telling us where you'll be." Susan added that she was almost ready to return to Pinkston's hideout looking for him, and Aunt Jenny said sharply that dinner would be in an hour. She'd just go put it in the oven, but then she lingered, not wanting to miss any of what Gus said.

The judge finally silenced them by putting two fingers in the corners of his mouth and letting out a loud, piercing whistle.

"Ladies, I'm sure Gus will tell us where he's been as soon as you quiet down, give him a beer, and let him sit a minute."

"I've got to call Jake. He'll be furious if he's left alone while we hear Gus' story."

Gus' protests that there was no story fell on deaf ears.

Susan called Jake, who was indeed upset not to be with everyone else. She mollified him by saying she'd come get him for supper, if he'd call Walt Wainwright.

"I better call Dirk too," he said. "Hurry on. I'm ready to go right this minute."

She hurried, but still it was almost forty-five minutes before everyone was settled in Aunt Jenny's now-crowded living room. The judge offered beer, Scotch, and wine all around. Both Wainwright and Jordan declined on the grounds they were on official business, but Susan gratefully accepted a glass of wine and refused to let Jake have Scotch, in spite of his pitiful plea. Aunt Jenny had finally put her casserole in the oven, and tantalizing odors were beginning to drift into the living area.

Wainwright was fatherly. "Now, son, you had us all in a dither. Tell us where you've been."

Gus looked at the expectant faces and wished he had a dramatic story to tell them, but the plain truth came tumbling out. "I took a friend to a doctor's appointment in Fort Worth."

"On a Sunday?" Jake was incredulous.

Gus looked down at the rug. "It was a doc-in-the-box."

Susan was too quick for him. "It was Amanda Meyer, wasn't it?"

He had no fabricated story ready at the tip of his tongue, so he nodded and said softly, "Yes."

Susan didn't let up. "She's carrying Jesse's baby, isn't she?"

Gus mumbled, "It's not for me to say. You'll have to talk to her."

Even Jake remonstrated, "Susan!"

Dirk was businesslike. "Gus, we're all worried about your safety. If you know you won't be someplace where we can easily check on you, please let ... let's choose Jake ...

please let Jake know. We don't want you to lose your independence, but we want to keep you safe."

"I understand, sir, and I'm grateful for the concern. I don't want to cause my mother any more grief."

Aunt Jenny sobbed, and Lucy rushed to her side.

Wainwright assumed his fatherly tone again. "Son, I'm between a rock and a hard place. I need to rid my county of drug dealing, and I can do that. But if I raid Pinkston's camp, we may never find out who killed your brother. I need to know, though, who all is in that cabin. Let's start with the women."

"They don't stay at the cabin, sir," Gus said. "The smell is so bad, they couldn't. They go to an apartment in town."

"Answers one of my questions," Jordan said. "Tell us about them."

He began hesitantly. "The dark-headed one is Rhonda. She's okay, been nice to me a time or two. But the blonde—calls herself Dawn—is what my dad would describe as a hard case. I think she wishes she were a man. She tries to be as tough as Pinkston. But I think she was sweet on Jesse. She was always angry, but she's worse since he was killed. I stay out of her way."

Jake and Dirk Jordan exchanged quick looks, but they were letting the sheriff lead the way for now, and they kept quiet.

"How many men out there?"

"There's always one, sort of a guard. And Pinkston spends most of his time there, when he's not in town harassing Doctor Hogan." Gus smiled at his own small joke, and Susan tried to smile back, but she didn't think it was funny.

"Squirrel kind of follows Pinkston around like a puppy dog—with apologies to Lucy—and otherwise there are three or four that come and go. They have apartments in town."

Jake interrupted. "But there were probably thirty people in that parade or protest or whatever it was."

Gus rubbed his hand across his forehead. He was obviously tiring of being in the spotlight with all these questions, and nobody knew it but him—he was concerned about Amanda's reception with her family and then his. But he soldiered on.

"Pinkston brought them in for the day from other cities—Fort Worth, Stephenville, Mineola. He knows a lot of people in what he calls 'the movement.'"

The law enforcement officers began to talk among themselves, with an occasional question to Gus, like, "There isn't any particular time of day we could go out there and find a skeleton crew?"

"No, sir. If Pinkston has a chance at a big shipment, they work around the clock. Nobody dares complain."

"Were you and Jesse part of that?"

"Yes, sir. Jesse because he thought it was exciting, me so they wouldn't find out I was a spy."

"You boys do any coke?"

"No, sir. Jesse smoked pot, but I think he was smart enough not to get into coke. He felt he had an obligation to finish college. He hated my dad, and I think finishing college was a way to rebel against him."

More discussion and then the big question, from Walt Wainwright, "Gus, do you think Pinkston shot Jesse?"

"Yes, sir, I do. But I got no proof."

Aunt Jenny bustled back into the room from the kitchen. "It's past six-o'clock, and I'm sure you men are hungry. Dinner's ready in fifteen minutes."

"I'm hungry too," Susan said with a laugh, "even though I'm not a man. And I know Ellen wants that chicken."

Ellen had stayed to hear what was going, partly out of curiosity but mostly because whenever she made a move to leave, she was showered with, "Don't leave," and the like.

Aunt Jenny frowned at Susan, as though to remind her feeding men came first.

The two lawmen excused themselves, and the others eventually gathered around Aunt Jenny's table, where talk was about anything but guns and Pinkston and Jesse. Nobody lingered after dinner. Susan and Jake headed for her house, and Gus was noncommittal about where he would go.

"Not to my parents' house," was all he would say.

Aunt Jenny fluttered and fussed but could not persuade him to stay in her guest room.

Susan, overhearing that, couldn't help a sly thought: if Gus stayed in the guest room, where would the judge sleep? One obvious answer.

When the house was empty and quiet again, Jenny sat motionless on the sofa, head bowed, hands folded in her lap, for so long the judge left his reading chair and sat beside her, putting a gentle arm around her shoulders.

"Jenny? Are you all right?"

"No. I'm scared . . . for Susan, for Gus, even for Lucy. Those awful people." She shook her head in disbelief that such people existed in her world.

"Jenny, I wouldn't want to scare you further for anything, but you must be cautious for your own safety. You, too, are in danger. Because of Lucy."

"I won't give Lucy up!" Her tone was fierce.

"I wouldn't want you to. I just want you to understand. I want you to stay safe in this house, with Lucy beside you, whenever I'm not here."

She nodded numbly.

* * * *

Next morning Jenny Hogan was her usual cheerful self, bustling about to serve the judge his breakfast of oatmeal with brown sugar, calling both Susan and Gus for reassurance that they were fine and receiving it, talking baby talk to Lucy until the dog rolled over on her back for tummy rubs.

"You know, John, the world looks much brighter to me this morning."

"I'm so glad, Jenny." He looked up from his oatmeal and smiled at her. "I have to go take care of a few things at my house this morning. You'll be all right here?"

"Of course, John. I'm just going to putter in the kitchen, decide what to cook."

"Sounds fine," he said. "Make me a grocery list if you need to."

She smiled and nodded.

After the judge left, Jenny Hogan did putter in her kitchen. She pulled out several recipe books and sat staring at them. Finally, she began a grocery list, having decided on a recipe, new to her. Lamb stew for supper.

Impulsively, she took off her apron, picked up her purse and headed for the grocery. She could easily have her shopping done by the time John returned, and then they could have a leisurely day at home, maybe go for a drive in the country.

She gave Lucy a lecture on good behavior, dropped a kiss on the dog's head, and left, carefully locking the door behind her. Jenny's old Buick was parked in the back of the driveway, because it was rarely driven these days, and she trudged back there, unlocked the car and got in, oblivious of her surroundings in spite of John's warnings. The car sputtered and spat but finally turned over. As she backed down the driveway and drove slowly down the street, she never noticed the car behind her.

Jenny Hogan was on the third aisle of her shopping expedition when she saw him—a man with a rifle, pushing an
empty grocery cart and, she was sure, following her. Her
heart began to race, and she felt her hands grow clammy.
She stole a quick look, then a longer one. This was the man
Susan called Pigface, she was sure of it. He had tiny eyes
almost buried in a puffy face and his hair was pulled into a
ponytail. There was that ugly black rifle slung over his
shoulders.

Feeling almost faint, Aunt Jenny wasn't sure what to do.
She didn't have a cell phone or she'd call John. She was
afraid the man would stop her if she tried to run. "Jenny
Hogan, that would be showing fear if you ran. You must
turn around and push your cart right by him. Take him off
guard by smiling and saying good morning." But she didn't
do it. Her knees were shaking too hard.

Slowly, a step at a time, she moved toward the checkout
counter. She desperately wanted to look behind her and see
if he was following, but she couldn't make her head turn
that way.

At the checkout counter, she emptied her cart of its six
items—toilet paper, a head of leaf lettuce, fresh strawberries
that probably didn't have any flavor so early in the season,
Lipton onion soup mix so she could make John's favorite
dip, potato chips, and a box of cereal, the dry kind with
fruit that John liked. She could hardly make stew—she
needed the leg of lamb, scallions, frozen peas, baby carrots,
tiny potatoes. She'd have to send John to the store after all.

She'd been so preoccupied she hadn't looked at the
checker, and she nearly jumped when a soft voice said,
"Miss Hogan?" Was it in front of her or behind? Had
Pigface come up behind her? Surely, he knew her name—
that thought alone sent a tremor of fear through her.

"Miss Hogan," the voice repeated. "Are you all right? You look pale."

She looked at the checker and let out a huge sigh of relief. "Oh, Gus, I'm feeling a little faint, I'm afraid."

"I'll get someone to take this cash register and help you out," he said quickly.

And then she remembered. "No, no, you mustn't. You stay right here." She jerked her head toward the line behind her, but when she got up the courage to look, Pigface wasn't in line. Had she imagined this?

"Miss Hogan, let's just get these groceries out to your car." Gus picked up the bag and offered Jenny his free arm.

Arm in arm, they went to her car, where she fumbled for keys and finally opened it. Once she was settled in the driver's seat, Gus leaned in.

"Are you sure you're all right? I can drive you home."

Jenny longed to accept his offer. What if Pigface followed her again? But she thought saying yes to Gus would be weak. She could and would drive herself home. After thanking him profusely and assuring him she has fine, she backed out of her parking space and drove slowly down the lane of parked cars. Looking in her rearview mirror distracted her so badly it nearly caused her to crash into the cars on the driver's side—Gus was talking to Pigface.

Gus' posture was stiff, his fists clenched, his expression intense, but Pigface was relaxed, almost insolent in the way he stood and the look on his face, as if he were taunting Gus.

Jenny was relieved she wouldn't be followed, but she worried about Gus. As soon as she got home, she'd call . . . but who should she call? Susan was at class, Jake should be resting. She'd call John if he hadn't already beaten her to the house.

He hadn't, and when he answered her call with "Everything all right, Jenny?" she lost her bravery, further undone by the annoying fact that John knew it was her before she told him. "I . . . I need you to go to the grocery for me." Her voice broke, and she sounded just what she said she was . . . needy.

She tried again. "I saw him. He followed me in the grocery store, with his gun. And I'm worried about Gus."

"Saw him who? And what were you doing in the grocery? How does Gus fit into all this?" He waited a moment, and then said, "No, don't tell me. I'll be there in five minutes."

When she poured out the entire story to him, John picked up the phone and called Jake, who asked what groceries Aunt Jenny had to have so badly that she went to the store alone.

"I'm looking at them. Toilet paper, lettuce, strawberries, onion soup mix, and potato chips. Won't even feed the two of us a decent meal, let alone you kids. She says I'm to go back for a leg of lamb for a stew . . . yes, I know it sounds wonderful. I'll let you know."

The judge turned to Jenny, who sat on the couch looking like a repentant child. Before he could speak, she said, "I just thought I'd save you a trip to the store."

He sat beside her and took her hand. "Jenny, look at me. I would rather make twenty trips to the store than have put you in danger . . . or have you feel threatened. Jake and I agree—and I'm sure Susan will—we don't want you to leave this house without one of us. We simply don't want you anywhere you are vulnerable. You're safe here." He reached for his phone and stood.

"I've got to call Gus and check on him."

The judge listened to Gus, getting little comment in himself, and then said, "You better come for supper tonight, son, so we can talk. I hear it will be lamb stew, if I get myself to the grocery quick enough."

As far as Jenny could tell, Gus acquiesced, because John said, "Give me the rest of the list, and then call Susan and Jake and tell them to be here for supper. We need to talk. While I'm gone, you keep the doors locked, keep Lucy with you, and stay away from the front windows."

"Are you trying to scare me, John?"

"Yes, if it will put some sense in your head. Go ahead and start the stew if you can. I'll be back with the rest of the ingredients as soon as I can. Maybe I can check on Gus while I'm at the store."

She didn't tell him she hadn't gotten any of the stew ingredients on her aborted trip.

* * * *

By the time Susan called from her office, John was back from the grocery and Jenny, cooking and in the kitchen where she ruled, had recovered her bravado. "Oh, Susan, it was nothing. Silly of me to be so alarmed. But you're right. He does look like a pig." She tried to laugh.

"Aunt Jenny, this is serious. We'll talk at dinner."

Chapter Eighteen

The lamb stew was delicious, all agreed, but Gus, not the stew, was the center of attention at dinner, though a reluctant star. But when Jake demanded to know what Pigface said to him, he was more talkative than any of them expected.

"He seemed to have forgotten about the night he tried to kill me. It was as though he thought I was still one of his followers. No threats, nothing like that. He told me he had an assignment for me."

"What did you say?" Jake asked.

"Nothing. I just waited for him to go on. He said he wanted that dog back"—Gus nodded toward Lucy, who sat at Aunt Jenny's feet— "no matter the cost. And he wants the collar and leash."

"The leash is long gone," John said. "I remember throwing it in the trash at PetSmart."

"Was the handle on the leash thick enough to hide drugs?" Jake asked.

"Maybe. Maybe somebody at PetSmart got a surprise. Did you find out how much what we found was worth?"

Jake hit his forehead with his hand. "No, I will. First thing tomorrow. What he'll do to get it back depends on how much it's worth."

Gus spoke up. "I don't know how much was just talk to impress me, but he sounded like he'd go to any lengths—including kidnapping or murder. Sorry, Miss Hogan."

Jenny gasped and grabbed John's hand.

"It won't come to that," Jake said. "What about you?"

"He implied that if I didn't make this happen, I might meet the same fate as Jesse." Gus' voice was low, and he refused to look at any of them.

The judge spoke up. "That may lead us a bit closer to what happened to Jesse. Suppose he refused to do something Pigface wanted."

Gus spoke slowly. "Jesse was an opportunist. If he thought it was to his advantage, he'd have betrayed Pinkston. He had no loyalty, even to his family. If he were going to do that, you'd think he'd warn me, but he never said a word."

"Time to call Wainwright in on this," Jake said. "We've as much as fingered Pinkston for Jesse's death, but I'll be damned if I know how to prove it." He punched a number into his cell phone and talked briefly with the sheriff, simply telling him about the stalking incident and the threat to Gus. When he ended the call, he turned to the others. "He'll be here in twenty minutes."

Gus looked uncomfortable. "I . . . I have someplace I need to be. Can you all tell him my part of the story?"

"I'm sure he'll want to talk to you, son." The judge clearly didn't think Gus should leave. "I don't think Pigface thinks you're a follower any more. I think he was just posing to get his hands on the coke. Once he got it back, you'd be . . . what's the word? Toast."

"Please, sir, this is important, and it may help. I'll come back, or I'll call the sheriff. Whatever. Give me an hour or so."

* * * *

Gus had no appointment nor commitment. He suddenly felt the need to find Amanda and make sure she was all right. He even thought she might know something that would help them. And he hadn't heard about the reaction of either set of prospective grandparents.

She wasn't in her room, but neither was her roommate, Jill, there, and Gus was relieved about that. He didn't particularly like Jill, and lately he was unsure of her reaction to Amanda's pregnancy. For reasons he hadn't even figured out himself, Gus desperately wanted Amanda to have this baby. He was afraid Jill would persuade her to get an abortion. It wasn't his faith that made him object—he thought maybe he wanted to have a little piece of Jesse on the earth.

He checked the student union. He knew Amanda often took her books and studied there, sometimes over a lonely meal. Jesse had been scornful of her habit of eating in the union where, according to Jesse, they served food fit only for a dog.

She was there, bent over a book, pen in hand as she scrupulously took notes. A half-eaten salad sat on the table.

Gus slid into the seat opposite her so quietly he had to call her name softly to get her to look up. "Amanda? Can we talk?"

When she did look up, relief flooded her face. "Oh, Gus. I am so glad to see you. I tried to call you this morning, but I guess you were at work and not answering. I have so much to tell you."

Boldly for him, he reached out and took her hand, holding it only briefly. "I want to hear it, Amanda."

The words poured out of her. Her father, as she predicted, had all but disowned her, while her mother stood by
and cried into her handkerchief. Amanda was not to darken
their door again, and they would not pay for her education
anymore. Her father scoffed that a girl with a baby didn't
need an education anyway. She might as well scrub floors.

Appalled at the man's harshness, Gus reached for her
hand again. "I can help you, Amanda. I . . . I have to find a
place to live, and you'll be welcome there. The baby, too,
when the time comes. I think . . . well, it's the least I can do
to make up for what Jesse did to you."

"I've been thinking about that," she said. "I don't suppose I'll ever forgive Jesse, but I don't suppose I'll ever stop
loving him with at least a corner of my heart. And now I'm
excited about the baby. It's not a burden he left me with. I
hope, boy or girl, it will grow up with a bit of Jesse's charm
to remind me why I loved him, but with your sense of doing what's right."

They were both silent for a moment. Gus relieved that
she wanted the baby so badly, and Amanda wondering how
to thank him for his offer.

"Gus, you're young. Once you're out from under your
father's thumb, you should date and be free. You don't need
to be saddled with me and, later, a baby."

"I've always been a bust at dating," he told her, "you
know that. Jesse was the ladies' man in the family. I've
had—what? —maybe three dates in my life, and they were
without exception awkward, miserable experiences. I don't
want to date, but I don't want to be alone. Now tell me
about my folks."

"Your father is convinced the baby will turn out to be
wild, reckless, just like both his no-good sons." She smiled
as she said it. "He's wrong, of course. I'll raise that baby
with all the love you boys never got from your father and

your mother wasn't allowed to give. I know from things Jesse told me when we were younger that if he even thought she was coddling you, he'd raise the roof. He was a strict disciplinarian, wasn't he?"

Gus nodded. The whole turn of this conversation had taken him by surprise. He wanted to protect Amanda, of course, but he had practically proposed to her. Not what he intended at all. "And Mom?"

"She was like my mom—crying, only this time from happiness. It's like she thought she'd have a bit of Jesse back by having his child near her. I think those grandfathers will come around when the time comes. I'm going to work on it. I'll meet my mom away from home, but I'll visit your folks every so often—he didn't tell me not to—so that they keep in touch with the baby."

Gus just sat and grinned at her.

"After this semester, I'll have to slow my education down, but I'll look for scholarships, and I'll get a job. Even if I can only take one class a semester, I won't give it up."

"Good for you. I'm sort of planning to go to school myself once this mess is cleared up."

"What mess? The baby?" She was alarmed.

"Oh, no. I'd never call your pregnancy a mess. I meant once Jesse's murder is solved and . . ." He realized she wouldn't know about the drugs and he couldn't tell her. "Uh, and a friend of mine is in some trouble," he ended vaguely.

Then he stood and said, "I want you to meet some people who are very important to me. Will you go to supper with me tomorrow and meet them?" That was bold, he thought, but then he was feeling bolder lately. He'd have to ask Aunt Jenny if it was okay to barge in on them like that. Maybe he could bring groceries. "One of them will feed you. I can tell you're not eating enough, probably not the things you need."

"You're preaching at me," she said as she closed her book and stood up. "Here, put this in the trash, please." She handed him the salad in its disposable bowl.

* * * *

Gus was apologetic when he asked Aunt Jenny about bringing Amanda to dinner, but she was immediately enthusiastic.

"Gus, of course, we'd love to meet your friend. Do you think she'd like beef or chicken?" If she thought theirs was a budding romance, she managed to keep that to herself. Gus told her chicken might best and then had no idea why he said that.

Then he got to worrying that Amanda would back out of her promise to go with him. He'd persuaded her to meet new people too easily. She was basically shy, and he was surprised that she didn't object, hesitate, even say no, she wasn't going.

When he picked her up that evening after work, she said all those things. "I'm just not ready to make small talk with people I don't know. My mind is still on Jesse and the baby and the future that scares me."

"Amanda, these people are different. They are the kindest, most caring people I've ever met. Not at all like your folks or mine. You'll see. But please come with me and don't be shy."

Reluctantly, she agreed.

At Aunt Jenny's house, Gus knocked, and the judge answered the door with, "Come in, son. We've been waiting for you. And who have you brought with you?"

Amanda smiled and held out her hand, but the words, "I'm Amanda," froze on her lips as she looked at the room that seemed crowded with people she'd never met. Gus made introductions all around, and Amanda smiled stiffly. She wanted to run, but she couldn't do that to Gus.

Then she was enveloped in Aunt Jenny's warm hug. "Come sit right here, young lady, and tell me all about yourself. I saw you at Jesse's funeral, and I'm so sorry for your loss. When is your baby due?"

Susan gulped, and Amanda blushed. Gus finally managed to say, "Amanda's expecting at the end of summer, maybe first of September. We plan to be in my apartment by then. We're both going to work and go to college." He didn't add that was the plan as of only last night, and it was still so new it had him reeling in shock.

Jake clapped him on the shoulder and said, "Well, you sly old dog, you."

Gus stood up straight and spoke clearly. "I don't want any of you to misunderstand. Amanda and I have known each other since we were little kids, but Jesse was her special friend. She's carrying his baby."

Amanda looked around at the faces, not sure what she expected—disdain, condemnation, even disapproval. She saw instead a warm welcome.

Susan came over and hugged her. "We've met, Amanda, but under less pleasant circumstances. I'm awfully glad to see you looking so well."

Aunt Jenny fussed over her more, and the judge said, "Now you just sit still, young lady, and tell me what I can get for you. No alcohol."

"Oh, no, sir," she stammered. "Could I have a glass of water?"

"Coming up," he said, and he headed for the kitchen.

Susan spoke gently to Amanda. "If you've known Gus all your life, you must have also known Jesse. How long have you and Jesse been . . . ah . . . romantically involved?"

Amanda looked at her levelly. "Ever since I was five, but I never knew Jesse really. Nobody knew Jesse well. Not even Gus. The fact that I'm carrying his baby doesn't mean I knew how his mind worked."

Jake spoke up. "I'm sure you'd like to see his murderer punished, but we're having a hard time with that. Did he ever say anything to you that would help us, give us a clue?"

"I knew about Mr. Pinkston and the drugs, if that's what you're asking," she said. "And days before he died—the last time I talked with him, as a matter of fact—he said Pinkston was angry at him, thought Jesse would betray him."

"Would he have?" Jake asked.

Amanda didn't hesitate. "Yes, he probably would have."

Gus spoke up. "I have to confess something here. I wasn't completely truthful about Lucy. I didn't steal her from Pinkston, though I wanted to. He was so cruel to her. But Jesse brought the dog to me and told me to keep her safe. And he added, 'Keep her collar and leash with her.' I guess he knew the secret of the collar. And he was double-crossing Pinkston."

Jake shook his head. "Motive and opportunity. But it's all hearsay. If you testified under oath, Gus, it might carry weight with a jury. But for a solid case against that man, we need proof—an eyewitness, fingerprints that we won't get because we don't have the rifle used to shoot the young boy. We're coming up empty."

"Rhonda might give you the answer," Gus said. "Dawn never would."

Without waiting, Jake keyed in Dirk Jordan's cell phone number. Then turning to the others, he said, "Jordan can at least question the blonde one that shot me. She's waiting on the grand jury. The other one has been released. Even if, as you say, Gus, she won't talk. He can try."

"What's for supper, Aunt Jenny? Can I help?" Susan suspected the others were getting hungry, and it was time to end this conversation.

"Oh, dear," Jenny said, flustered by the talk. "There's a chicken in the oven, roasting with potatoes and carrots. And green beans on the stove. I'll just go get it on the table."

Susan followed her aunt to the kitchen, and Amanda followed, as soon as she could free herself from Lucy, who had crawled up in her lap in spite of remonstrance from the judge.

"May I set the table?"

Knowing a chore would make her more comfortable, Susan said, "Of course. Thank you," and pointed out the flatware drawer, napkins, and everything else needed.

"Amanda," Susan said, "I'm curious. Tell me about Jill. I have a feeling she wasn't telling me all she knew about Jesse. And it wasn't just that she thought she was protecting you."

Amanda dropped the silverware noisily on the table in surprise, but when she found her voice she spoke forthrightly. "No, Jill is all about Jill. I've always known that. She only drew the line at dating Jesse because she was smarter about him than I was. But she knew about the drugs, bought some pot from him. Will she get in trouble?"

Susan shook her head. "Not unless you complain to Jake or the sheriff."

Amanda smiled just a bit and went back to setting the table.

Dinner turned out to be quite satisfactory, the chicken crisp on the outside, moist on the inside. With them all gathered around the table, the meal turned into a quiz-Amanda hour, but Amanda sensed theirs were caring questions. She answered truthfully about her future plans, confessed that the plan to stay with Gus had only come up yesterday, and that she would take Gus up on his offer for the sake of the baby.

Gus blushed and added, "That's why I'm doing it. I'll be an uncle to that baby. I have family responsibility there." Then he added, "Plus, I would worry about Amanda. She may have been Jesse's girl, but we've been friends a long time."

Talk turned to the fact that they were all convinced Pinkston killed Jesse but couldn't prove it.

"That's really frustrating," Jake said, slamming his fork onto the table harder than he meant.

"Rhonda would tell you if you can find her," Aunt Jenny said, and Susan sensed her sixth sense was kicking in again. She *knew* Rhonda would tell them. "Seems simple enough to me, and Gus says she's a good person."

"I didn't exactly say that, Miss Hogan, but she's a lot nicer than Dawn. It might be worth a try, but somebody'd have to find her in town, maybe tail her to wherever she's staying." He was thoughtful for a moment. "I've seen her in the store a time or two. I guess I could do that—at least find out where she goes. Then the sheriff could find her to talk to her. He sure can't go to that cabin, until he's ready to make one grand raid."

"Gus, that's too dangerous," Jenny protested. "Who knows what she'd tell that Pigface fellow."

"I don't intend for her to know I'm following her," he said with a slight grin. "I hope I'm better at tracking than that."

Jake jumped in. "I think it's chancy, friend. Amanda has given us even more reason to want to keep you safe. I wish I was up to doing it myself."

"You're not," Susan said firmly. "But I am, but I'll be careful she doesn't see me. After today, she'd recognize me.

Gus, any time she usually comes in? I may have to do a lot of shopping."

Aunt Jenny had her mouth open to object, but Jake beat her to it. "Susan, I absolutely will not have you chasing around town after one of Pinkston's people. If she doesn't know you, he does. And I know you—you'll take the whole thing into your own hands."

He regretted his words as soon as he uttered them. Susan Hogan did not like to be told what to do, and she'd see not his words as an order or even a request, but a challenge. He looked directly at her, but she refused to meet his look, and her jaw was clenched.

The judge addressed Gus. "Son, if you came into my courtroom and testified that you got that collar from Jesse and didn't steal it from Pinkston, I'd be inclined to believe you. But if the sheriff even thought it was a backup possibility, it makes your safety all the more important. You've got to let us protect you."

"At least," Jake broke in, "Pinkston doesn't know the sheriff has the collar. He still thinks Aunt Jenny has it. He won't harm Gus as long as he thinks Gus can get it for him."

Gus shuddered a bit, but it was John Jackson who spoke. "That's true, but the person that really puts in the bull's-eye is Jenny." He turned toward her. "Jenny, I can't stress how important it is that you make sure one of us is with you at all times."

Jenny muttered, "Oh, fiddle faddle."

"No fiddle faddle," the judge said. "We mean it. I'm here most of the time, and if I have to leave I'll call for backup."

"I'll call the doctor tomorrow and ask if I can drive. I feel a lot better." As if to demonstrate, Jake stood and did a little soft-shoe dance.

Susan frowned, and Aunt Jenny, smoothing her hair, protested, "I'll be all right. No one needs to protect me."

Jake stopped his dance. "Aunt Jenny, if you don't agree, I'll forcibly take you to a gun control class and make you learn to shoot."

The older woman threw her hands up in the air in a gesture of resignation.

Chapter Nineteen

When Susan got home from her classes the next afternoon, Jake greeted her pathetically. "Doctor says I can't drive yet, no matter how good I feel. I need you to drive me somewhere." Then, like a little boy, he added, "Please?"

Susan was wary, her voice full of caution. "Where?"

He grabbed her hand. "Come on. We're going on an adventure."

"I haven't gotten over the last one." But she grabbed her purse. Susan was usually ready for any adventure Jake suggested. Lately, though, he hadn't suggested many, and she was leery of the word.

"Jake, tell me where we're going." Without an answer, she steered him to the passenger seat and climbed into his truck, watching while he hoisted himself in carefully. The old swinging casually onto the seat was gone, at least for now.

"I'll tell you where to turn." He shook his head, as she backed out of the driveway and followed his directions to head out into the countryside.

"Jake, I can't drive without knowing where I'm going."

He remained silent. They drove many miles, or so it seemed to Susan, until finally he directed her to pull onto a dirt lane with an unmarked mailbox. At the far end, she could see a modest white farmhouse, probably clapboard siding, and a couple of outbuildings that all looked well maintained, even if the road wasn't graded. As they bounced closer to the house, she heard barking—a lot of it.

"Jake Phillips, you've brought me to a kennel."

"Yes, ma'am. Guilty as charged. But there's a twist."

"Twist?"

"This is a rescue kennel. They save abandoned, abused, lost animals from shelters, find 'em new homes. If they're tagged or have some form of identification, they try to find the owner. Operates mostly in a four-county area."

"So much for getting a puppy." Hadn't he said he wanted to train a puppy and hadn't she pointed out he didn't have time?

He pounded on the dashboard in frustration. "Dammit, Susan. I'm trying to compromise here. I know you don't want a puppy, and I don't have time to train it. I called out here today, and they've got a couple dogs I want to look at."

In that instant Susan saw that a dog was inevitable in her future, and she could either accept it happily—she did love Lucy, didn't she? —or she could resist, ruin her relationship with Jake, and make everybody, including Aunt Jenny and the judge, miserable. She chose to accept. "What kind of dogs?"

"A lab, a pittie, and . . . I hesitate to tell you this . . . a standard labradoodle."

"I want to see that one first."

"Nope."

The kennel owner, an older lady with gray hair caught casually at the back of her neck and wisps flying loose all around her face, came out to the truck. As she walked up to the open window, Susan saw skin deeply creased by too much West Texas sun and blue eyes sparking with kindness. She wore blue jeans that had been worn a lot, and a blue jean jacket, also faded and worn, over a T-shirt that Susan couldn't quite read. She imagined it said something about dogs.

"Jake? I'm Ella Briscoe. Welcome to Second Chance Kennels." When she discovered Jake wasn't in the driver's seat, she talked across Susan to him.

"Second Chance? You don't have a sign." Susan didn't even wait to be introduced.

"No, ma'am. We don't want everybody in the world to find us. Only take referred people, like yourself. Howdy. I'm Ella. And you?"

Why did this woman make her stammer? "I'm Jake's . . . uh, partner."

The eyes twinkled. "Good. Then it will be your dog too. You like dogs?"

All sorts of answers ran through her mind from "Not at my house" to a gushing "Oh, yes." She decided on neutral. "I've never had a dog, but I think the one my aunt has is pretty sweet."

Ella looked from one to the other. "You want sweet," she nodded at Susan, and turning to Jake, "you want guard dog. Hard to find that combination." She turned business-like. "Park over there under the oak tree, and we'll go look."

As Susan maneuvered the truck, she asked, "Who recommended us?"

"The judge. Who else? Not Buster Conroy, I can tell you that."

For a minute, Susan had almost been able to put Jesse, Gus, Amanda, Pigface, the whole mess out of her mind. Jake's one mention could ruin the day if she'd let it. The dread washed over her again. "I probably am like you," she managed. "I want a guard dog."

They followed Ella to the kennels and without asking she took them to one of the larger kennels and showed them the labradoodle. "This is Gracie. She's got a sad story—well, all of them do—but Gracie was abused and lost that wonderful trust in people that seems inborn to labs. She's still afraid of a lot of people, and she lashes out when she senses someone she can't trust. But what impresses me is that she has a fine sense of who she can trust and who she can't."

With that, she opened the kennel door and stood back. Gracie emerged slowly, looking Jake and Susan over. Then she planted herself in front of Jake and sat, like a dog who had just been given the "Sit" command.

Jake reached a slow, gentle hand toward her and let her smell it. She sniffed, and then nuzzled the hand. In a minute, she stood and sidled up to him, pressing against him.

Susan stood uncertainly. *What if she decides she can't trust me? I'll die on the spot.* But she called Gracie's name, and the big dog—seventy pounds, at least—walked slowly toward Susan's outstretched hand. She sniffed, turned to look at Jake, and began to lick Susan's hand. The next minute, Susan was on her knees, arms thrown around the dog, who nuzzled her neck.

Susan looked up at Jake, about to speak, but he spoke for her. "You don't have to say it. She's our dog."

Ella was grinning, but she said, "I have the other dogs you wanted to see."

"No need," Jake said. "I think Gracie has made our decision for us."

* * * *

Within twenty-four hours, Susan declared Gracie the perfect dog.

"Because she spends all her time on your lap, where she doesn't fit." Jake looked at Susan, sitting on the couch with the dog half sprawled on the couch, half on Susan, and legs dangling in an ungraceful manner.

Jake fixed Susan with a serious look. "If we get married and then split up, would we have joint custody?"

Jake had spent the day with Gracie while Susan was at school and had only relinquished her attention reluctantly. They'd walked, played catch the Frisbee in an empty field, practiced commands—she knew sit, stay, come, heel, and down. He'd thrown food on the floor and told her to "Leave it." She did. And then he'd released her with an "Okay," and she daintily nibbled his treat.

"She's had training," Jake exulted, "even if it was harsh."

"Do you suppose someone beat her?" Susan hugged the dog.

"I know they did," he said matter-of-factly. "Now come on. Aunt Jenny's expecting us for supper—smothered pork chops with mashed potatoes. I'm starving."

"Have you fed Gracie?"

"Of course. I don't want her fighting with Lucy over food."

"Will they get along?"

"Yes. Gracie is older. She can help teach Lucy."

"Teach her what?"

"Susan, would you please just call the dog and get in the car?"

He still didn't have his doctor's permission to drive, so Jake insisted they go in the car with the dog, partly because the truck was his work vehicle and he didn't want dog hair all over, but mostly because he still hated for Susan to drive the truck when it wasn't necessary. Gracie rode in the back

seat in Susan's Honda, sitting erect, nose over the seat between Jake and Susan.

"She needs a seat belt," Susan ventured.

"I can order one from Amazon. Quicker and easier than
going to Fort Worth to PetSmart. Meantime, hook her
leash around the seat belt back there."

Susan was apprehensive about this meeting. What if the
dogs didn't like each other? Neither seemed to have a
fighting disposition, but you never could tell.

Her fears melted when she saw the dogs together. They
sniffed each other from head to toe, although Aunt Jenny
scolded Lucy for butt-sniffing Gracie, and John said, "Let
them be, Jenny. They're dogs—contrary to what you think
most of the time."

When Gracie growled at Lucy for getting too close,
Aunt Jenny rushed to comfort Lucy.

"She's teaching her manners, Jenny. Go in the kitchen
and fix our dinner." His words were harsh, but his tone affectionate.

Sybil the cat viewed both dogs with distaste and disappeared into Jenny's bedroom.

Lucy lay at Aunt Jenny's feet and Gracie at Jake's while
they ate supper. Susan considered tempting Gracie to her
side of the table with a morsel of pork chop, but she knew
both men would scold her.

"I really want to see about this instinct for bad guys Ella
said she has. I'd love to test it, but the bad guys I know
wouldn't put up with it."

Judge John's eyes twinkled. "You could go out to
Pinkston's camp. She'd find plenty of candidates."

"Nope. I'll just let it happen naturally," Jake said.
"Might pick up on an undetected bad guy in Oak Grove."

And that's just what happened, only the bad guy wasn't
exactly unknown. Floyd Pinkston had the nerve to ring

Susan's doorbell the next day. Jake answered, with a firm hold on Gracie's collar. The minute he opened the door to see Pinkston's round face, Gracie growled, a low rumbling sound that began deep in her chest and worked its way up until it was a threatening bark. Jake knew the difference of a bark of excitement and one warning of danger. He held firm to the collar.

"Whoa, man! Can you control that dog?" A rivulet of sweat ran down the man's face, and he wiped at it with a graying handkerchief.

"Yeah. What can I do for you?" And, to the dog, "Good girl."

Gracie kept up that deep rumble in her chest.

"I keep hearing rumors about a dog like mine being seen in this neighborhood . . ." He backed away nervously. "I guess it was a mistake. Folks must've meant this dog."

"Must have," Jake agreed and closed the door. He watched Pigface retreat, crossing the lawn, glancing back at the house occasionally in puzzlement. When he was safely in his car and had driven away, Jake indulged in a good laugh.

Then he called Wainwright and reported what had happened.

Wainwright said the expected things about, "Sounds like a good dog. I'd like to see her. Nothing better than a fine dog. Did you get her because you wanted a dog or for protection?"

"Both. I wanted a dog, and I wanted Susan to have protection when I'm not here."

"When you going back to work?"

"At least two weeks." It stretched like an eternity to Jake. He was keeping up with emails, phone calls, and things he could do by computer, but he itched to be in the office. Even then, he'd be on restricted activity—doctor's orders, reinforced by Susan.

Wainwright chuckled again. "Listen, I went by the jail and visited with that woman who calls herself Dawn. Got nowhere. She's a hard case, won't crack. I asked outright about Jesse Conroy, and she about spit in my face. Said he was a kid who shouldn't have been there, didn't care about Pinkston, had threatened him."

"I bet Jesse's threat wasn't a threat at all but something he did—stealing the dog and collar."

"I think that's probably what happened," Wainwright said. "I won't bet against you. But we can't prove it. Gus is our best hope. Wish he'd do a better job of lying low."

* * * *

Little did Wainwright know as he spoke, Gus was wishing he had taken the lying-low advice more to heart.

Pinkston and Squirrel walked boldly into the grocery, carrying their weapons in their hands rather than having them over their shoulders.

"Looking for Conroy," Pinkston growled at the nearest checkout clerk. "Call him. Tell him Pinkston is here to see him."

When Gus got the message, he was in the storeroom and quickly considered his options. Then without a word to anyone, he bolted out the delivery door at the back of the store, not even stopping to grab his phone, and began to run through back streets in the neighborhood behind the store. As he ran, he tore off his stained white apron, figuring it marked him as both a target and a store employee. He's pay them for it later. He was not, he told himself, fool enough to face Pinkston, nor did he want a showdown in the store. He ducked behind garages, even trash cans, when he heard cars coming.

If I keep going this direction, I can make it to Miss Hogan's house and call for help.

He was a block from Aunt Jenny's house when he heard a bullet whine way too close to his head.

Damn! But they drove here, then waited for me, so I didn't hear a car.

He ducked behind a construction dumpster and then, spurred by fright and a desperate need for self-preservation, climbed into the dumpster and pulled the lid shut. Crouched carefully on the building debris—sheetrock, boards with nails, a sack of plaster in powdered form that gave him an uncontrollable urge to sneeze—he waited and listened, trying to quiet his heartbeat, which sounded as loud as a jackhammer to him. Pigface no longer wanted information from him. Gus knew he wanted vengeance. He wanted to kill him.

Pinkston and Squirrel never investigated the dumpster directly. He heard them walk around it, talking big to each other about what they'd do to him when they caught him. Then they moved off, and he could hear them some distance away, calling to him, as though they thought he'd show himself.

"Come on, Conroy. We just want to talk. Promise we won't hurt you."

Yeah, and I've got oceanfront property in Arizona to sell you. How stupid do they think I am?

Eventually, the voices faded and disappeared. Gus Conroy stayed in that dumpster until dark, praying that no one dumped a fresh load of old lumber on top of him. He even dozed a bit, but the fourth time he cautiously raised the lid, he was greeted by darkness. Climbing out, he landed on the ground on both feet but lost his balance and tumbled into some soft mud. Once he was upright, he took inventory. He was muddy, dusty with plaster, and ravenous with hunger.

Can't go to Miss Hogan's like this . . . but I don't have a choice.

* * * *

Back at Gus' store, a sobbing cashier told his manager the story of two men looking for the assistant manager with rifles in hand. "They . . . they just looked mean. And they didn't have their rifles over their shoulders like usual. You've seen 'em in here before, I know you have."

The manager, Rick Johnson, put her story together with Gus' sudden disappearance and called the Oak Grove police. The dispatcher immediately put him through to Lieutenant Dirk Jordan, who came out to the store in person, with two officers with him. They interviewed Rick and the cashier, and then he put out an APB on Pinkston and Squirrel and a memo to all officers to watch for Gus, who needed protective custody. Jordan alerted both Wainwright and Jake, knowing word would then spread through the community.

By late afternoon, Jake and the judge were out together, in John's pristine car, driving the streets of Oak Grove, with Gracie seated erect between them. Jake didn't mind if she got dog hair all over someone else's car. It was the least of his worries now anyway, and even the judge didn't protest the dog's presence. They made three useless passes by the Conroy home and once checked with Buster Conroy at his shop. When told his son was missing, the man just shrugged and turned back to the car he was working on.

Dirk Jordan called Jake's phone to report his officers had found Pinkston and Squirrel, sitting in Pinkston's ratty old car parked on Oak Grove's Main Street. "Hauled 'em in for questioning, but they claimed to be running errands.

We had no evidence to hold them. Their rudeness at the store isn't a crime. Maybe should be."

"At least," the judge said, "they didn't seem to have Gus. Did anybody check with Amanda?"

"No," Jake said and they headed toward the campus. He stayed in the car while the judge went into the dorm. After what seemed to Jake an inordinately long time, the older man came back out, shaking his head. "All that did was upset her, too. We have to call her the minute we find him."

* * * *

Susan and Aunt Jenny were huddled in Jenny's living room, each trying not to worry the other and both desperately afraid for the young man they had become fond of. Susan was acutely aware that except for Lucy and the locks on the doors, they were virtually unprotected.

She called Jake and began the conversation on an accusatory note that immediately made him defensive. "You didn't leave Gracie at home by herself, did you?"

"No, Susan, she's in the car with me and John."

Susan moved to the kitchen, so Aunt Jenny wouldn't hear her. "Sorry, I'm just edgy. I wish you'd bring her here. We're sort of unprotected. I don't think Lucy has the idea yet."

"Better yet," he said. "I'll bring John. He's armed."

"No," Susan said. "Just bring Gracie. You can't drive around alone, and you know it."

"Susan, for Pete's sake, I'm okay." Exasperation showed in his tone. "How long are you going to force me back into invalid status?"

"Until the doctor dismisses you," she said crisply. "Bring the dog. Please." She knew his adrenaline was flowing right then, but she also knew he'd collapse in exhaustion sooner or later.

It was fifteen minutes before John appeared at the door with Gracie. "I think you're right, Susan. I can serve best by sticking with Jake. We'll keep in close touch."

"Thanks, John."

Gracie didn't seem to mind being handed off. She settled down by Susan and growled softly at Lucy if she approached. If the young dog lay by Aunt Jenny, Gracie was perfectly content.

Both women tried to read, since conversation seemed out of the question. It wasn't long, though, before Susan threw her magazine on the floor, startling Gracie. "Aunt Jenny, we've had no word. You know what they say, 'no news is good news.'"

"I never believed that," the older woman said, dabbing at her eyes with a tired Kleenex.

Susan stood up decisively. "What's for supper? I'll get it started."

Shaking her head, Aunt Jenny said hopelessly, "I have no idea. See what you can find in the freezer."

Improvising meals was not one of Susan's skills, but on the theory that anything was better than just sitting, she turned to the freezer, which yielded a pound of ground meat, some hamburger buns. The refrigerator gave her celery, the cabinet held a can of beans and a can of diced tomatoes, and there were onions hanging in a wire container by the sink. With the help of a recipe she found on her computer, she cobbled together a mixture she could call sloppy Joe, seasoning it with Worcestershire, A-1, and white wine in the absence of the red wine called for.

She had just put her concoction in the crockpot to warm, when a loud crash brought her running to the living room. Both dogs were barking, and Aunt Jenny was crying. Susan started with her aunt, getting her to sit back down and speaking soothingly until Jenny subsided into sobs.

She managed to say, "My window—again. Susan, see what's broken this time. Was there a bullet?"

By now the dogs had stopped barking, but Gracie was fixated on a large rock on the carpet, with a note wrapped around it.

Susan's first thought was, *So not original.* Her second thought was to call Dirk Jordan and then Jake, in that order. Jordan, as she knew he would, ordered everyone away from the rock until his men got there with an evidence kit. As far as she could tell, the rock missed the lamp on the front table and did no other damage beyond the window itself.

Susan could keep herself and her aunt away, but there was no moving Gracie. She was giving it her undivided attention and that deep low growl that came from far down in her chest. She almost seemed to think it was some living creature, and she watched to see that it didn't move.

Jordan arrived and echoed Susan's thought. "Couldn't Pinkston come up with something we haven't read about in a thousand novels?"

Aunt Jenny was wringing her hands. "It's the second time I've lost my front window! But please read the note. It may say something about Gus."

It didn't. It was an outright threat about people getting hurt if that dog collar wasn't put out on the front steps by midnight.

"Well, that makes it easy," Jenny said. "We don't have it, so we'll simply put out a note telling him that."

"I'm afraid that won't do," Jordan said. "But they'd be fools to come check at midnight. We'll be waiting, just in case."

Jake and the judge came back, dispirited but hungry, and Jordan left, saying the women were in good hands now. Susan had called the local hardware, given them a sob story, and they had boarded up the window, with a promise to be back tomorrow with new glass.

Susan's sloppy Joe met with a lukewarm response that had nothing to do with the quality of the food and everything to do with the worry of those eating. Conversation was almost nonexistent, and Susan resisted the urge to contribute light patter. They ate in silence.

As Susan was scraping plates, Lucy went to the back door and began whining insistently.

"Lucy, it's okay. Come on in the living room." Aunt Jenny tried to pull the dog away from the door, but Lucy resisted and kept whining.

"Aunt Jenny, stand back. I'm going to open the door and see what's upsetting her." Jake's handgun was at the ready.

He cautiously opened the door and then flung it wide, giving out a joyful shout. "Come in here, young man. You look awful!" And with that he ushered a disheveled, dirty Gus into the kitchen.

The first words from Gus were, "Miss Hogan, I am so sorry to come here looking like this. I . . . I didn't know where else to go."

Oblivious of his dirt, grime, and plaster dust, Aunt Jenny rushed up and hugged him. "Come in and sit down in the living room. Susan will bring you food."

"I can't sit on your couch like this," he protested.

"Yes, you can," Aunt Jenny said. "I can get the couch cleaned. We want to hear where you've been, and why you look so awful." She practically pushed him down to the couch and then seated herself beside him, making it plain she wasn't budging for anything or anybody.

Jake appeared with a glass holding two fingers of bourbon.

"Oh, I don't drink whiskey," Gus protested.

"You need it tonight," Jake said, forcing the glass into his hand. "Sip it. I've got to go call a certain young lady who's worried about you . . . as we all were."

Gus blushed to the roots of his hair. "I'm fine. No need to make a big deal out of it."

But when he recounted his afternoon adventure, they all sat spellbound and finally announced it was a big deal. Jake called both Jordan and Wainwright, telling them they might want to hear this tale.

When they arrived, Gus had to repeat the whole chain of events, recalling one more time the endless hours spent in the dumpster. It was plain that he was exhausted.

"Son," Wainwright said, "you did the right thing. If you'd gone out to the front of the store to meet those men, you might be a dead man by now."

Gus paled, though the sheriff wasn't telling him anything he didn't already know.

"I'm taking this man to my house and putting him to bed . . . after he has a shower," Susan announced.

"Susan, wait! We've got to plan some strategy. We can't let those men continue to terrorize our town."

"You don't need Gus or me. Plan away, gentlemen. And tell me about it in the morning." Taking Gracie with them, she and Gus moved toward the door. Gus was full of apologies and offered to stay if they needed him. Susan simply said, "Jake Phillips, you remember what the doctor told you. Don't get tired. Someone will bring you home."

To her astonished embarrassment, he again said, "Yes, Mother. I'll come right home."

"Oh, dear, I'm going to bed too." Aunt Jenny was less tired than she was running from the conversation about to take place in her living room.

* * * *

Ten o'clock the next morning. Aunt Jenny's driveway was empty, except for her ancient Buick. The house had an empty air about it—no lights except for one dim one in the living room. But the curtains were open, and someone observant could see Aunt Jenny sitting on the couch, book in hand, head slumped as though dozing. No one else appeared to be around.

Looking all around, two men—Pinkston and Squirrel—walked up the driveway, carrying rope, duct tape, a hammer, and handguns. Their rifles were slung over their shoulders, and their expressions were cautious, though one gave the other a thumbs-up sign.

If anybody had been watching, the furtive air of the men would have aroused suspicion, but apparently no one was watching. The back door stumped them for only a minute—sliding glass doors, not secured with a stick in the track and easily gotten off track to allow passage into the kitchen.

As soon as Floyd Pinkston set foot in the kitchen, a flying, growling ball of fur leapt at him from the far corner of the room. Gracie clamped her jaws around his gun wrist and began to shake her head back and forth.

Pinkston screamed in pain, dropped his gun, and yelled frantically, "Get it off! Get the damn dog off me! Squirrel, do something." The more he writhed and twisted, trying to shake the dog loose, the harder Gracie held on. Pinkston was flinging blood all around the room, and in his desperation, he knocked a full coffee cup off the counter, sending the contents spraying everywhere.

Finally, Jake, gun in hand, came forward and commanded, "Gracie, off. Good girl." The dog sat obediently, and he bent to pick up the dropped gun.

Pinkston collapsed in a moaning heap on the floor, clutching his wounded arm and demanding medical care.

"I'll sue. I'm crippled for life. My gun hand is ruint." He babbled, making empty threats.

Jake nudged him with one toe. "Shut up."

Pinkston was immediately quiet.

Squirrel thought the back door his best option, but the voice of Dirk Jordan stopped him. "Don't even think about it, cowboy."

Squirrel froze, raised his hands in the air, and whined, "Keep that dog away from me. I got a turrible fear of dogs."

"Good to know," Sheriff Wainwright said. "I'll remember that. May hire that dog." He looked at Jordan. "Not sure which one of us gets the privilege of his company, but we better call EMTs. Haven't had a man die in custody and don't want to start now, even with this scum."

Jordan punched his phone and spoke briefly, then said EMTs were on their way and his men were stationed around outside, not that he expected any trouble. "I'll bow to you, Wainwright. You got the murder charge, and that outweighs mine of breaking and entering."

"Murder!" Squirrel screeched, now handcuffed to the chair in which he had been unceremoniously seated. "I didn't murder no one. Pinkston did it. This whole mess was his idea—the drugs, killing Conroy, kidnapping the old lady."

"Shut up," Pinkston growled. He was still clutching his arm, but he had quit moaning and had begun to recover enough to think about the situation he found himself in.

"Won't do any good now, Pinkston," the sheriff said. "Cat's outta the bag, you might say."

"That witch," Pinkston muttered. "It's all the old lady's fault. If I could just get my hands on her for five seconds, she'd learn not to mess with me." Then, slowly, something dawned on him. "Where is she?"

Jake came back into the kitchen, carrying a mannequin that had been padded with pillows and had a gray wig and spectacles. "Meet Miss Jenny Hogan."

"No fair. You tricked us," Pinkston complained. "Won't stand up in court."

"Don't bet on it," Dirk Jordan said. "Especially since we videotaped everything from the moment you stepped across that threshold. Want to call your lawyer?"

EMTs at the front door cut short Pinkston's reply, and Jake went to let them in. They were careful, efficient, and showed Floyd Pinkston more compassion for his pain than any of the other men in the room. They got him up off the floor, seated him in a chair at the kitchen counter, and used the counter as a surface on which to bind the wound. The bleeding had slowed but it still made a mess.

"We doped him up a bit," one told Wainwright. "You probably need to take him to the ER to be checked out. And don't take anything he says serious for about six hours."

"Lawyer! I want a lawyer!" Pinkston begged.

"You get a phone call. Got your lawyer's name and number?"

"I don't have a lawyer," he muttered. "Never got caught . . . never needed one before. I want one of them court-appointed ones."

"Me too." Squirrel had been silent and might better off have stayed that way.

Wainwright turned to him. "We'll get you a lawyer. You're charged with breaking and entering, and I'm sure other charges will come up, like attempted kidnapping. A policeman will take you to the jail, while I take this, uh, man to the hospital."

"He done it all," Squirrel said. "I just done what he told me."

"Start with your real name, please."

"Luke. Luke Tompkins."

"Good, I'll run it and see what I come up with."

An officer grabbed him roughly by the elbow and escorted him out the back door. Wainwright was only a bit gentler with his wounded prisoner.

After they left, Jake said, "I have to call Susan—ten minutes ago."

"Tell her not to bring her aunt home until we get this mess cleaned up."

And that's how the Oak Grove chief of police and the university chief of campus security ended up on their hands and knees, scrubbing up blood and coffee.

Epilogue

It was a lazy Saturday morning. Jake and Susan were having breakfast on her deck.

"The grand jury indicted Dawn for assault with a deadly weapon and assault with intent to kill," Susan said.

"I know. Why bring that up?"

"I want to know why she shot you. And what happened to Rhonda?"

"Susan, why are you so interested in these women?"

She stretched, stood, and paced. "I don't understand the whole thing. Why were they here? Why choose Oak Grove for an open-carry protest?"

"Because it's a college town. Open carry was a cover. They came to sell drugs on campus, and the two women came because they were infatuated with Pinkston. As for why Dawn shot me, I think it's like why she made that anonymous phone call. She was proving herself to Pinkston, for all the good it didn't do her."

"Gus knew about all of it and didn't tell. Will he get in trouble?"

"I doubt it. Wainwright, Jordan, and I will all speak on his behalf. Susan, do we have to keep talking about this? I'm going out to my house today. Can I take Gracie with me?"

"No. Are you moving back to your house?"

"No. But I need to go check on it. Can't I take her? If we were married, could I take her?"

"What difference would that make?" She looked at him with disbelief. "She's my dog."

"If we get married and then split up, would we have joint custody?"

About the Author

In 2014, award-winning novelist Judy Alter introduced the Oak Grove Mysteries featuring Susan Hogan and Jake Phillips. Three years later, Alter hopes readers remember Susan and her scrapes with both the law and death after a coed on the campus of Oak Grove (Texas) University is murdered. If not, she suggests you start with *The Perfect Coed*.

Judy began her career writing about women of the nineteenth-century American West, and her fictional biographies— *Libbie, Jessie, Cherokee Rose, Sundance, Butch and Me, The Gilded Cage*—are available as e-books. Around 2011, she turned her interest to the cozy mystery genre, joined Sisters in Crime, and within seven years published eleven mysteries. *Pigface and the Perfect Dog* is her twelfth outing in the genre, and, no, it is not a young-adult title, though some teens, knowledgeable as they are these days, may enjoy it.

In addition to the two Oak Grove Mysteries—*The Perfect Coed* and *Pigface and the Perfect Dog*—Alter's mysteries include the seven books in the Kelly O'Connell Mysteries series: *Skeleton in a Dead Space, No Neighborhood for Old*

Women, Trouble in a Big Box, Danger Comes Home, Deception in Strange Places, Desperate for Death, and *The Color of Fear;* three in the Blue Plate Café Series—*Murder at the Blue Plate Café, Murder at the Tremont House,* and *Murder at Peacock Mansion.*

Her work has been recognized with awards from the Western Writers of America, the Texas Institute of Letters, and the National Cowboy Museum and Hall of Fame. She has been honored with the Owen Wister Award for Lifetime Achievement by WWA and inducted into the Texas Literary Hall of Fame and the WWA Hall of Fame.

Judy is retired as director of TCU Press, the mother of four grown children, and the grandmother of seven. She and her dog, Sophie, live in Fort Worth, Texas.